DEVIL'S SPAWN

by

Tex Larrigan

Dales Large Print Books
Long Preston, North Yorkshire,
BD23 4ND, England.

British Library Cataloguing in Publication Data.

Larrigan, Tex
    Devil's spawn.

        A catalogue record of this book is
        available from the British Library

        ISBN 1-84262-113-0 pbk

First published in Great Britain 1995 by Robert Hale Ltd.

Copyright © Tex Larrigan 1995

Cover illustration © Faba by arrangement with
Norma Editorial S.A.

The right of Tex Larrigan to be identified as the author of this
work has been asserted by him in accordance with the
Copyright, Designs and Patents Act, 1988

Published in Large Print 2001 by arrangement with
Robert Hale Ltd.

Dales Large Print is an imprint of Library Magna Books Ltd.

Printed and bound in Great Britain by
T.J. (International) Ltd., Cornwall, PL28 8RW

DEVIL'S SPAWN

After the Civil War was over it dawned on Tom Hitchens that he'd made the biggest mistake of his life when he'd chosen to follow Ben and Josh Kirby on a vengeance trail against the Yankees. The head wounds Josh had sustained earlier were becoming a problem, and he deteriorated into a wild beast, lusting after women and shooting them afterwards. Tom had plenty of blood on his hands but now he yearned for the time when he could hang up his guns. First, though, he had to resolve his differences with the Kirbys ... and survive.

ONE

The four men huddled beneath the shelter of the trees as the rain lashed down, their thin-flanked horses pawing nervously. They were drenched and their grey Confederate uniforms showed black. One of their number took no interest in the curling smoke coming from what was once a cookhouse but was now just a ramshackle shelter. He was slumped over his horse's neck, only vaguely aware of the rain and the cold, for the blood ran freely from a great gash running from his temple to his cheekbone.

One of the other men looked at him and frowned for it was to be seen that the boy, for he was no more than twenty, needed treatment and quickly.

'Courage, Josh. We'll soon have your head

attended to and we'll have food in our bellies by the look of that smoke.'

The boy tried to raise his head to acknowledge his brother's words but it flopped again. His eyes closed. If he hadn't been lashed to his horse, he would never have come this far.

They were fugitives from the battle of Perryville in that October of 1862, and they'd been part of Colonel Quantrill's troop of guerrillas and under the command of General Braxton Bragg, God's curse on him for a fool, Ben Kirby thought as he considered his kid brother. He cursed Bill Quantrill too, for being the low-down bastard he was, lighting out with most of his guerrillas and leaving the wounded and stragglers behind. So to hell with the Confederates and Quantrill. The war was going badly anyway and it was a man's duty to think ahead. If Josh survived, then they would do as Quantrill did, prey on whoever it took for them to survive and to hell whether they were Confederates or Yanks.

They were all the same under the skin!

The oldest man of the bunch looked at Ben.

'You want Tom and me to do a recce? I can't see that there'll be much danger. Mebbe a lone woman or some old folk. But it sure smells good, whatever's in that pot.' He sniffed appreciatively at the smell of beef stew cooking.

Ben didn't answer but nodded and the two men cantered off while he turned his attention to his brother.

'Josh, can you hear me? We'll soon have you off that horse and a slug of something inside you to warm you through.'

He looked with concern at the boy. Josh was probably the only person in the world he had any feeling for. Most of his feelings had died when he found the remains of his father's homestead in ruins and his other brother and father shot in the back of their heads and his mother and sister raped until they'd died of it.

Young Josh had escaped for he'd been out

hunting a lost mare and foal and he'd come back in time to see the Union soldiers eating and drinking their food and liquor and playing games with his mother and sister.

It had been too late to help his family and so he'd hidden out until the troop had finally packed up and moved out. But his mother and sister were dead.

Ben had come home wounded from the war and found a shocked Josh living by himself like an animal. He'd cried for the first time when Ben put an arm about him. He'd aged from a naïve farm boy to a bitter man with the one idea of finding Captain James Brockenridge and killing him with his bare hands.

Ben realized that Josh's mind was unhinged and that to watch over him he must take him back as a recruit to his own troop.

They had never come to clash with James Brockenridge and now it was probably too late. He was sick of the misery of the war, the privation and the hunger and the whole damned stench of it. He wanted out of it.

His mind was made up. He and Josh and the two trusted comrades, Tom Hitchens and old Grizzly Jones would do what Quantrill was good at. It was time they got the biggest share of the pie.

He was interrupted in his thinking by the sound of hoofbeats and he looked up to see old Grizzly Jones coming back. He had a wide grin on his bristly face.

'We're in luck, boss. There's an old man and a woman living in that shack and they're shit-scared of us. Tom's watching them. You can bring the young 'un in, no problem.'

Ben grunted in satisfaction and proceeded to lead Josh's horse in to what was left of a small barn.

Swiftly he haltered the horse. The poor devil's bones showed for lack of food and hard riding. He would have to forage later or they would have dead horses. But now, the priority was getting Josh inside out of the rain and his wound cleaned and bound up.

Josh slipped sideways when his legs were unbound. Ben took his weight and gathered him up and took him inside the shack. It was dark and smoky and for a moment or two he couldn't see and then he made out a small scrawny woman with grey hair scraped back into a knot and wearing either a black or dark-grey dress and a dirty apron. She crouched over a black iron pot slung over an open wood fire. Beside her on a rough wooden bench sat her gaunt-faced husband, his gnarled workworn hands gripping his knees as if to still their shaking. Tom stood over them, his army pistol nonchalantly at the ready. But they did not offer any resistance. They were pitifully frail.

Ben's nostrils flared. The stench of un-washed bodies, woodsmoke and the unmistakable smell of blood was nauseat-ing. Ben's eyes wandered over the crude shelter and located a makeshift bed.

'You there,' he said, pointing his chin at the old woman, 'pull the blanket back off the bed so I can lay my brother down.'

The old woman gave a gap-toothed grin and pushed hair out of her eyes.

'It's already taken, mister, if you'd look properly.' She went on stirring the stew.

Ben motioned to Tom.

'Have a look, and see if she's telling the truth.'

Tom pulled back the blanket and then gave a yell.

'Hell! There's a dead one here and he looks as if he's been dead a week!'

Ben cursed and lay Josh gently on the dirt floor and then straightened and flexed his muscles and went to the farthest corner of the room and peered down at the body. He spat on the floor to clear his throat of the sudden upsurge of gorge in his throat. He saw that the corpse wore only a vest and long johns. No clue as to whether he was a Confederate or a Union man. He turned to the old couple.

'Who is this man and when did he die?'

The old woman still grinned and stirred her stew. It smelled burnt.

'Well?'

The old man stirred himself and spoke heavily.

'Our son. He came home to die just as that young feller is aimin' to do. They all come back to die.' He stared hard at Ben.

'Was he a Confederate?'

'Of course. Aren't we all in these parts?'

'Then that old woman of yours won't mind tending this boy's wound?'

'You'd better ask her yourself. She's crazy, you know. Hasn't stopped stirring that stew since the day our boy died. It's not fit to eat.'

Grizzly Jones wrenched the iron ladle out of the woman's hand and scooped up some of the stew, his guts rumbling at the burnt but meaty smell. He tasted the gravy and grimaced and spat it into the fire where it sizzled and gave off an acrid steam.

'Jesus! He's right. They must be sitting here starving themselves to death. I wonder if there's anything else to eat around here?'

The old man's laugh was about as crazy as the woman's.

'The Yankee bastards took everything we've got, burned down the boss's house and killed the family. They didn't even leave us a chicken and if it wasn't for the fact we had this piece of beef hidden in the creek yonder, we wouldn't have that.'

Suddenly he started to cry.

'There's no one left here but us. It would be a blessing, mister, if you shot us both. We're too old to start again!'

Ben looked at them both and nodded, considering. Then without further ado he shot the woman between the eyes and before the old man could voice his thanks, he slumped with a bullet through the brain.

Josh stirred and Tom gasped.

'Did you have to do that?' Tom asked, suddenly sick to his stomach.

'You heard him. He wanted out. It was a kindness. Look around and see if there's anything clean enough for a bandage and we'll get Josh trussed up and when the rain clears we'll be on our way.'

'But the boy's all in. We should stick it out

until he's rested.'

Tom showed some concern, but Ben showed no signs of letting up.

'Look, this is no time to be soft. We've come this far and we've dodged General Don Carlos Buell's mopper-uppers. If you fancy your chances in a Yankee jail, I don't! Josh is coming with me and you and Grizzly can please yourselves!'

Grizzly, who had been silently listening said softly, 'I'm with you, Ben, all the way. If we can get into Kansas and ditch these uniforms we can head west for the Indian Territories where there must be good pickings.'

Ben nodded. 'What about you, Tom? Are you staying up here and risking being caught by either side? You're either a prisoner of the Yankees or a deserter of the Confederates. You can take your pick because you're going to get picked up sooner or later, that is if you don't stop a bullet first!'

Tom was reluctant but he knew Ben was a

good leader. Better in a group than travelling alone.

'Yes, I'll go along with you,' he said slowly, heavily. Ben was a good leader but he was ruthless. Dragging his own brother along when he looked to be half dead. He looked up at Ben. 'Can we not stay till morning? We were expecting to. There's no danger here now. The Yankees are long gone.'

'What? Stay here with this lot? No. We'll fire the shack and get away and to hell with it!'

Tom turned away and went to tend Josh who was muttering in delirium. There were beads of sweat across his upper lip and his skin felt cold and clammy. It looked as if it would take all of Josh's youth and strength to live this night.

TWO

'The bank's been robbed!'

The cry went up from those walking along the Main Street of the small township of Barr's Creek in Kansas. At once pandemonium reigned. Men and women scurried for shelter in shop doorways and in the saloons and the curious peeped and watched the two riders who, with rifles at the ready patrolled in front of the bank. Any fool who moved in would be dead on the instant.

The townsfolk of Barr's Creek were well versed in hold-up procedures for this same damn bunch had had the cheek to part the bank from its gold reserve amounting to $50,000 not a year ago and the bastards had disappeared into the hills.

From then on, the Kirby gang had struck in several Kansas townships but it was only after a bank manager had been shot and killed and the reward had been anted up to $2,000 for each man, that the gang had been treated with the respect it enjoyed now. The four men were reputed to be all dead shots, trained during the Civil War with Quantrill's guerrillas.

They were now famous, most of the details of their respective lives having been highlighted in the small-town journals.

But this hold-up was a little different. Joshua Blundell, the owner and manager of the bank in question, had been full of hell at the last visit. He'd sworn on the grave of his dead wife that that particular group of bastards would never get away with it again if they ever came back.

Now was the time to try out his plan.

Suddenly there was a hell of a bang inside the bank and the two riders outside wheeled their horses and each snatched the reins of the tethered mounts as planned for a quick getaway. Then, Tom Hitchens, suddenly worried about the unusual report that sounded like gunpowder, prepared to dismount and join in the fracas inside but was saved by the bank door being slammed open and Ben Kirby, and his brother Josh, staggering out amidst a suffocating cloud of smoke and an acrid smell of cordite.

Choking and cursing, the two brothers forked their horses and, with a rebel yell, all four men thundered along the street and on out of town along the narrow winding stage road.

At once, the brave men of the town came out like rabbits from their burrows and the owner of the store across the way entered the bank to find out what had happened.

He found the banker covered in blood, a victim of the blast from his own booby-trapped safe. The safe door hung askew, and the contents, apart from two bags of coins, were just burnt ash.

But Joshua Blundell was alive and he wanted revenge.

'Get the sheriff and tell him to arrange a posse. There's a reward of five thousand dollars for the men who get those bastards, dead or alive, and that's apart from the government reward,' and he gasped and flaked out unconscious.

So the hunt was on. Sheriff Jordan wasted no time in deputizing a dozen men who were lured into a gruelling ride into the hills for the sake of not-so-easy-earned cash. They followed the trail along the narrow winding road until they came to a fork and turned naturally up into the hills. There they were stymied and wasted time hunting for sign and Sheriff Jordan cursed for Tommy Twofeathers, the halfbreed scout was not with them. He'd taken off the day before to go and spark his wife before she got sick of living alone and took up with some other brawny stallion.

Josh Kirby laughed wildly and took the lead from Ben while Grizzly Jones and Tom Hitchens followed behind. Ben had the brains but Josh was the one who took risks. It was as if he didn't care about life or death.

It made no odds with him. He was a dangerous man to cross and his temper uncertain. Josh had changed mightily since that Yankee wound to the head. He'd also filled out and no one would describe him as a naïve farm boy any more.

His reckless air and his undoubted charm when things were going right for him, drew the saloon women. He was also generous. The more cash which passed through his hands, the more outrageous he was with his women. Easy-come dollars trickled through his hands like water. No matter how Ben remonstrated, Josh would only laugh and say that coins were made round to go round.

He was the one who was always broke and urging the others to another strike. He favoured the bullion trains, but Ben leaned to the banks. But this time even Ben had second thoughts. Once it got out that the Kirby gang had been foiled by a booby-trapped safe, all the bankers would be trying it. It also made Ben feel a fool, that he and his men took the risks and then galloped like a bunch of crazies out of a town with nothing to show for it.

Josh thought it funny and yelled and laughed like the maniac he was fast becoming but the laughter kindled Ben's knot of anger yeasting away inside him.

'If it wasn't for you, we shouldn't be in this position now!' he snarled. 'In future you'll only get a half-share of any proceeds you're due, and the rest is stashed. Understand?'

'Now to hell with that, big brother! I'm a big boy now and if I want to live it up I will! No question. Live for today is my motto. I'll never make old bones!'

'Stop acting like a piss-proud kid then if you're such a big boy. Your irresponsible actions are a danger to us all. I never wanted to go back to Barr's Creek. It was you and your bloody bleating on about keeping our hand in, that was the trouble!'

'Aw, shucks! You were counting the cents too, and Tom and Grizzly were all for it, weren't you, fellers?'

Tom hawked and coughed. He never liked being dragged into the brothers' arguments. He was becoming increasingly nervous about the way Josh was acting. It was as if Josh needed to live on the edge of disaster. It was as if he extracted nourishment from danger.

'I didn't object, Josh, because I knew it would be no good.' He might have added that it could be dangerous to go against Josh in anything he wanted to do. It was taking Ben all his time to control his brother and he, Tom, wasn't going to gamble with the boy's temper.

'See, Ben? What about you, Grizzly?'

'Well now, I'm game for anything. I've had a good life and more cash in the last three years than I've ever had in my life. Who am I to object?'

Josh laughed cockily at Ben.

'So! What do you think of that, Ben? You're not getting cold feet, Brother? I think you're getting a mite too cautious. We've got a reputation to keep up!'

'Now you can put those big ideas out of your mind.' Ben reached to poke the dry sticks on the small fire they'd allowed themselves to brew their coffee, while their mounts rested and grazed.

They had kept up that first headlong gallop until the sun had begun to set and then, when the horses showed signs of distress they had left the right-hand trail which Ben had chosen on a whimsy, thinking that if any posse was following they would naturally turn up into the range of hills running south. Not that he expected a posse. Most sheriffs objected to man-hunting beyond the bounds of their own township.

Ben was weary. His bones ached more often these days. He slept lightly and couldn't remember a good night's sound sleep since before he'd joined in the Civil War 'way back.

They drank coffee and tightened their belts. Food would come later. Ben reckoned an empty belly made a razor-sharp mind.

They hunkered down to rest but Ben's anger still kept him awake. The owlhoot trail was a good trail to follow if there wasn't a bloody fool in the bunch. Ben faced the fact that his own brother was the weak link in the chain. He would trust Tom and Grizzly until the death. His own brother – and he was startled at the thought that slipped into his brain – it might have been better for him and the others if Josh had never survived that night they fired that shack and burned those corpses before they crept through enemy lines and took the owlhoot trail...

He considered his brother, the little 'un whom his pa and ma had doted on and spoilt rotten by his dead brother and sister. The man he had become no way resembled the cheerful, helpful young teenager he'd been before Ben himself had gone away to join the Confederates leaving Josh and Dave to help out on the farm and help protect the womenfolk.

He faced facts squarely.

Josh witnessing the torture and death of

their folks had lost his soul. That and the head wound had wiped out all normal feelings. He doubted whether Josh had any real feeling for him. He was beginning to think that Josh saw him just as a leader and one who might get in the way.

He was going to have to have a private word with Tom about his brother, he came to the conclusion. Tom was steady, maybe not so enthusiastic when it came to the killings, but he had a cool head and, even if he didn't approve of the savagery that circumstances often warranted, closed his eyes to what he didn't want to see and never threw it up afterwards. Tom was all right.

Tom maybe would have an idea what to do with Josh.

Ben slept lightly and toed the others awake a couple of hours before sunrise. Again they drank coffee and Josh grumbled. Starvation was bringing out the beast in him. He needed hot food and he also needed a woman. He'd had disturbing dreams the night before, and they'd left him feeling weak and frustrated.

Ben kicked sand over the remains of the fire.

'Quit squawking. We all suffer, even old Grizzly. Now get mounted up and we'll do a fast burst and get out of this part of Kansas. I think it's time we headed farther west and set ourselves up 'way out in the territories.'

'Aw hell, aren't we going back to Jonty's place? I'll sure miss Molly.' Josh winked at Tom who didn't respond.

'Jonty's had more than enough out of us and I've a feeling about him and those arse-lickers who hang around him. How come the last four raids we've planned have turned out like damp squibs? Two of 'em had no real money in the safes and one of 'em had been raided in the same manner as we planned. I think there were big ears among that crew. I've been figuring it out. No, we're going to make our way west. They say that since the war ended there's a boom in cattle. Anyone can go and round up wild cattle and make a fortune...'

'You mean for us to … work?' Josh laid emphasis on what was a hated word.

'No, you fool! Use your head! Where there's fortunes, there's banks and gold! Stands to reason. There'll be more rich folks down there than there ever was in Kentucky or Kansas. We'll get more than pickings if we put our brains to use.'

'Aw, I don't know…' Josh began but the usually silent Tom put his spoke in.

'Looks like a mighty fine idea, boss. You know, if I could scrape some real cash together, I wouldn't mind settling down with a good woman and raising me some kids.'

Josh spat disgustedly.

'Hark at him! Tom's growing soft! Whoever heard of owlhooters settling down? You'd miss the excitement, Tom, and the minute anyone cottoned on you were slick with a gun, you'd be challenged, especially if there was a price on your head as there is now!'

Tom's fleeting dreamy look hardened.

'Yeh, you're right. Once an outlaw always an outlaw.'

He turned away to attend his horse and look her over for saddle sores and foot rot. Ben watched his back, a prickly feeling of awareness making him uncomfortable. How long would Tom last? Had he made a mistake about Tom, and was he going to be the weak link in the chain, not his crazy brother Josh?

'Well, what about it? For all we know there's a posse behind us.'

Josh laughed. 'A posse? After all this time? They've lost us for sure. No, they'll have done enough riding to satisfy the townsfolk and that old sheriff will have paid off his deputies and they'll all be drinking in the saloon and patting each other on the back and telling each other what good up-standing citizens they are!'

Ben grunted. 'I hope you're right. Still, we'll have to make a decision. What's it to be? Finding a new place to hole up in these parts or moving on west?'

'I don't care where it is as long as there's women to be had.' Josh rubbed his hands in anticipation.

'Oh, God, can't you think of anything but women? You keep your brains between your legs, boy. Don't you understand? We hole up private like, not in any outlaw nest with all the trimmings! We're on the run. Do I have to spell it out to you?'

Josh's scarred face flared red and, jumping to his feet and landing in a gunman's crouch, he went for his gun. With lips curled back from his teeth, he shouted passionately, 'Look, I'm not your little boy, you get that straight, Brother! I'm sick of your superior attitude and the way you try to run my life! If I want a woman I'll have one. Just because you can't...'

His words stopped abruptly as Ben's fist made a roundhouse twirl and connected with Josh's jaw. The boy rose in the air, arms thrashing, and slumped to the ground. Ben stared down at him for a long moment and then his eyes lifted and locked with Tom's.

Tom, turning quickly had heard everything and was just in time to see the punch.

'I think you did wrong to hit him, boss,' Tom opined. 'He's not the one to forget.'

'I know, Tom. What are we going to do with him? It's like looking after a wild animal.'

Tom shrugged.

'He's your brother. If he was mine, I'd take him and dump him in the wilds and find him a woman who could take the piss out of him. That's his trouble, boss. He's a frustrated stallion. Of course, we could geld him...' His lips barely twisted at his own joke for suddenly it seemed a good idea.

Ben's response was to scoop up Josh into his powerful arms and carry him off in the direction of a small stream. Tom heard the splash and then the scream. He smiled to himself. That should shrink Josh's nuts but he wouldn't like to be in Ben's boots!

Grizzly eased himself into a better position under his tree and scratched amongst his whiskers. He tipped his hat farther over his head and said in a hoarse voice, 'Tom we can look out for trouble. Them two will kill each other before the year's out. I'll take a bet on it.'

'Done. Ten dollars?'

'Yeh. One of us is bound to better himself if those two bastards snuff it. Tom?'

'Yeh?'

Grizzly sat up and removed his hat altogether, and his bald pate glistened in the moonlight. 'You know what?'

'No. What?' Tom saw that now Grizzly was real serious.

'Josh isn't the only crazy one. I've noticed Ben acts crazy too, you know, in small ways. He holds it back but one of these times he's going to snap and if that boy riles him too much…' His voice tailed off and he nodded significantly.

'You mean he would murder his own brother?' Tom's incredulity made his voice squeak.

'Yeh, I mean just that and by the look of 'em both, it could come at any old time.'

'Hell, Grizzly, I think you're wrong. Ben Kirby can kill, we've both seen it happen, many times, but his own brother...? No matter how crazy that young fool gets, he's the one person Ben cares about. Not you or me. We could go to hell, but Josh ... no, I think you're wrong.'

Grizzly shrugged.

'Well, time will tell who's right, and the bet's still on.'

'Right!'

They both listened to the continued argument going on in the undergrowth but suddenly it was over as Ben manhandled a flailing Josh back to the small fire and Josh shook himself furiously like a mad dog.

'I'll get you for this, Ben!' shouted Josh. 'Just see if I don't!'

'Aw, grow up and quit your bawlin'. You remind me of a lost calf...'

Tom put a warning hand on Ben's shoulder.

'Let him be, boss, or you'll send him over the edge!'

For a moment Tom thought Ben was going to argue and then he nodded.

'Yeh, you're right. We'll let the kid dry out and then we'll ride at daybreak.'

They hunkered down to sleep again, heads on saddles but neither Tom or Ben slept much what with Josh muttering and cursing and Grizzly snoring fit to saw wood and their own personal thoughts.

Tom was pleased at the sight of a new day when the first rays of light came over the horizon. He was up and watering his mount well before the others stirred.

He had made his decision. He would ride with Ben Kirkby until his stake was big enough to break loose. Then he would put the whole goddam vicious past behind him. Somewhere there would be a place for him where he could make a new start. He was only thirty-seven years old goddammit! And somewhere there could be a woman...

He didn't dwell on that fictitious woman for those kind of thoughts caused disaster and turned a man into a beast like Josh. He could do without that kind of self-torment.

Ben spoke little as they made their way ahead. He was moody and mean and Tom and Grizzly allowed the brothers to ride together as they walked their horses up and into the hills.

It was Grizzly who spotted the cloud of dust way back in the valley. He swore which alerted Tom who had been brooding on his future.

'What is it, Grizzly?'

'A posse if I'm not much mistaken. Look!' Tom looked back in the direction Grizzly pointed. Then he kneed his horse and caught up with Ben and Josh, Grizzly following close behind.

'Hey boss, we're being followed!' Ben cursed and kneed his horse about to have a better look. The horse pranced and it took time for Ben to focus. Silently he watched a string of riders come into view as they followed a trail down into the valley which they'd travelled the day before.

'Goddammit! They're on to us. By the way

they're travelling they'll be on us if we don't shift our arses!'

With that, Ben dug his heels into his horse's ribs and the mustang lunged and whinnied and then set a pace that the others had a hard job to keep up with.

That pace could not last long even though the mustangs were hard fit despite their thin flanks. A night's rest and graze had topped them up and Ben reckoned that they were more than a match for the tired horses of the posse.

They dismounted to traverse a steep slope and walked their mounts to aid heaving flanks. At the top of the slope they paused to look back. The posse's cloud of dust was still behind them.

Ben cursed.

'They sure are a persistent bunch! They must have put up the ante. I wonder how much we're worth?' He grinned suddenly. 'How about us holing up at the top of this draw, catching our wind and ambushing the bastards?'

Tom's heart went cold. He knew he was a fool to hope that the killing might cease when they got out of their home territory. Killing a posse would alert every damn sheriff and marshal right across the western states right down into Mexico! There'd be no hiding place once they got that kind of reputation.

'Does it have to come to that, boss?' His tone was brusque, his jaw tight.

Ben gave him a considering look. Now more than ever he was having second thoughts about Tom.

'What do you suggest then?'

Tom shrugged. 'I know we're in new territory but we could cut east and double backover and fox the bastards...'

'And play hide and seek and us without a bite to eat? Where's your brains Tom? Or have they become addled?'

Tom looked sullenly at him.

'It could mean big trouble.'

'Who the hell will know what happened to them? Anyone could have ambushed them.'

'That posse came after us. Everyone in Barr's Creek will know what's happened if they don't come back. We could even have a posse waiting at the first town we hit! The telegraph acts fast these days.'

'We'll have to take our chances. If those bastards have got an Indian scout with 'em, then they'll not let up. It's them or us. What you say, fellers?' Ben looked at Josh and Grizzly.

Grizzly scratched his chin. 'Seems like we have no choice.'

Josh whooped like a big kid given the OK to go to the fair. 'What we waiting for then?' he yelled. 'Let's get us some shelter and get down to some ambushing!' With that he led his horse away and a few minutes later gave a rebel yell. 'Wha'dya know, there's a pretty snug cave back here that looks as if it's been used some time.' Ben and Grizzly followed swiftly while Tom lagged a little behind.

The cave showed signs of use. Long-dead ash and sooted walls showed that up above was a draught chimney, a natural crevice, probably gouged out thousands of years ago by constant running water. Now the cave was dry, a veritable fort.

Ben laughed. 'A good omen, eh? If we had grub we could withstand a siege. As it is, those bastards will never know of this place. It's well to keep it in mind. Now let's fan out and find ourselves vantage points. Two of you on the far side of the trail and Josh and me on this side. With careful management, we can take the lot of them. Do as we did with Quantrill, make every bullet count!'

Tom hunkered down behind a rock which allowed him to watch the trail they'd made for a distance of at least three miles, he opined. There would be plenty of time to warn the others as they slowly climbed the rocky escarpment. They would probably walk their horses to save them as they had done. It would be like knocking off clay pipes at a fair.

His guts rumbled. If he didn't eat soon, he'd be reduced to eating grass and ants like the Indians. He sat quietly thinking and watching, waiting.

He thought he could smell salt pork. Christ! He must be in a worse state than he suspected. The scent faded and he reasoned it was because he'd been thinking about food. He'd better keep his mind on that posse. He hoped the continual climb upwards would eventually send a grumbling bunch of men homewards. He wasn't looking forward to killing in cold blood. After all, during the war, they'd been shooting at an enemy. These fellers were only men willing to protect what was their own. He'd do the same if he was a settler and had cash stashed in the bank.

The smell of pork came stronger now and Tom realized it was because the wind was stronger. He swore and stood upright and faced into it. He could swear it was real, and then he was stumbling and climbing up and over a series of rocks and found they were part of a rim and he was looking down into a green valley. He snatched off his hat for fear of discovery.

'Well, I'll be damned!' he swore softly to himself as his eyes took in the small log cabin, the corral, the few herded cattle and the grazing horses.

He saw the figure of a woman leave the cabin and carry a wooden bucket to a small stream that looked like a snail trail from his distance. She walked quickly and with long strides. She stopped to pick some flowers and she smelled them before tucking them into her waistband.

Tom smiled. She must be a young 'un to do that!

Then his attention was taken by a rumble of displaced stones and he chanced a look back over and he saw far down below at the beginning of the steep climb a bunch of riders.

Scrambling back to his vantage point, he gave a low whistle which was answered. They were ready. All they had to do was wait and watch and count the opposition and then blow them apart...

THREE

Tom carefully raised his head and watched from his hiding place. Ben had acknowledged the warning and, with Josh, was waiting. Grizzly too was ready, a little to Tom's right. He counted the men scrambling up the incline, their mounts objecting and struggling. It was going to be an all-out massacre in a few minutes.

Twelve men! They represented the fittest and most experienced menfolk of Barr's Creek. If they died, then there would be an all-out hunt for the killers.

Tom made up his mind. A shot before they reached that crucial point of no return and where they could find shelter was the answer.

He debated. They might turn and run and he and the others could make the most of the respite and disappear into the hills. He would then have to face Ben and a vengeful Josh and the chances were that unless he could talk fast, he was done. But to hell, he couldn't live in their shadow forever.

He took careful aim just in front of the sheriff so that his bullet should hit the rock and shower both man and horse with blasted fragments. It would cause pandemonium at the very least. He closed his mind to the outcome and fired.

It was as he figured. The horse leapt high in the air, dragging the sheriff, and the men and horses coming behind bunched and tried to scatter.

At once, Ben and the others went to work and Tom saw a horse with its reins entangled in its rider's arm, plunge and fall away down the escarpment, dragging its rider with it.

Then he was firing to save his own life. The bullets came thick and fast as the possemen leapt for cover, their maddened horses free to scramble either upwards or down and generally getting in the line of firing. The screams of frightened animals and of those injured and rolling away in the sudden sweep downwards, plus the blast of gunfire, filled the air. There was no time to think.

Tom saw two possemen rear up, splashed scarlet, and scrabbling to save themselves from the downward plunge, targets of Ben and Josh. Then Grizzly's gun roared twice in quick succession and two more men slipped to their deaths.

Tom felt sick. It was like killing sitting ducks. He blazed away and deliberately missed. He wanted none of this. Then suddenly he was facing Ben whose face was twisted in hate.

'You bastard! What in hell do you think you were doing? You fired too soon. We could have got the lot. I should kill you for this...' Ben was scrambling up his side of the track, so mad that he took no notice of what was happening around him.

Then Tom saw the gunman taking slow

deliberate aim at Ben, and Tom instinctively fired. The man flew backwards, bouncing with sickening thuds against the rocks below, and Tom was reaching downwards to give Ben a helping hand. He pulled him up beside him and, breathless, Ben sank down beside him.

'I owe you, but I should still kill you,' he gasped.

Tom stared down the track. It was unbelievable. Five men were thundering away back the way they'd come. The rest ... well they wouldn't be going anywhere.

'It's over. See, they're heading back to Barr's Creek.'

'There should have been none going back!' Ben spat and glared at Tom. 'Why did you do it, Tom?'

'I don't know what you're on about, Ben. I thought they were getting a bit close.'

'I'm the leader, Tom. You should have waited for me.'

'We're not in the army now, Ben. I did what I thought was best.'

'So you think you would make a good leader, eh?'

'No, I never thought that and you damn well know it! I just thought it the right time to set things going.'

'I'm not sure about you any more, Tom, but this time we'll let it go.' Tom breathed a sigh of relief. He was lucky this time but there was going to be a day when there would be a confrontation. He knew it deep down in his heart and it would be soon.

He remembered the valley over the rim.

'I've got a surprise for you, boss. If you climb up and look over the edge all nice and careful, you'll see what I've seen.' And that, he thought hopefully, would put all suspicion out of his mind.

He was right.

'Hell! It couldn't be better,' Ben said, scrambling back to Tom and grinning widely. 'Come on, let's holler for the others and we'll get right down there and get us some food!'

When Ben told Josh, his face lit up.

'A cabin down there? That means food and maybe a woman too. What are we waiting for?' And Josh was scrambling away quickly to find his horse with Ben close after him.

Grizzly spat in the dust when told.

'We'll have to go in quiet like. We don't know how many's holed up there.'

'Aw, shurrup, Grizzly, you old misery-arse; you always think the worst,' Josh's clear young voice bounced and echoed.

'And you, watch it, Josh. If anyone's going to make trouble for us, you will!'

'Hell, I wasn't the one who made the mistake of firing too soon and giving them bastards warning!' Suddenly all the suspicion was back and Tom went rigid, cursing the big-mouthed Josh to himself. Even Grizzly was looking at him with silent speculation in his eyes. Josh's eyes spat fire. 'How about it, Tom? Has that yellow backbone of yours gone soft?'

Tom glared at Josh, his right hand hovering over his Colt .45 while Josh seemed to slump into a crouch, his hands twitching over his guns.

'I'm neither yellow nor soft, Josh, and if you want to try me, get started,' Tom answered in a low clear voice.

Ben looked from one to the other, noting Josh's excitement and Tom's coolness.

'Calm down, Josh. Tom's just saved my life. It was just a mistake of judgement, wasn't it, Tom? You made a mistake?'

Tom hesitated, but what the hell...

'Yeh, you might say that, a mistake of judgement.'

'Then that's it, Josh, you shake Tom's hand and he'll forget what you said.'

The two men looked at each other and then Josh laughed and broke the sudden tension.

'He can forget what I said, but I'm buggered if I shake hands!'

Ben frowned, but Tom just turned away and adjusted his horse's stirrups. This business wasn't over yet. Josh would niggle on and the more he did and the more times Tom backed down the more cocky the young bastard would become. Tom didn't like it, but he was a brother of Ben's and shooting Josh would make him an enemy he could do without...

They skirted the rim of the valley and finally found a gap which Tom suspected might be an old Indian trail down to the valley floor.

They fanned out and came upon the cabin from the rear. There was no sign of life. All was quiet except for the grazing animals and the long lazy swirl of smoke rising from a crooked tin chimney.

They stopped and Tom leaned forward on the pommel of his saddle thinking of the woman he had seen. Perhaps she was alone?

Ben cautiously moved forward but nothing happened. He waved to the others and rode around to the front, Tom staying in the rear and Josh and Grizzly taking each side.

'Ho, the house! Anybody home?'

The answer was a shot-gun blast which fortunately for Ben expelled itself into the air above him, but Ben's horse danced and nickered while Ben cursed.

Then an old man was standing at the open door, the shot-gun poised and ready.

'Don't come no nearer, stranger, or next time you'll get it in the guts! Who are you and what do you want?'

'Never mind the who. We want food and water.'

'We? Who the hell's we?' Grizzly and a broad-smiling Josh broke cover and joined Ben.

The old man scratched his chin.

'I ain't got enough food for the lot of you. We ain't got much of anything right now, m'son's gone to get supplies.'

'We? How many of you in there?'

'Myself and…' He stopped as a youth of about sixteen shoved him aside.

'You stop talkin', Granpa. We ain't got nothin' so be on your way. We ate the last of the hawg and we only have flour and beans, enough to last until Pa returns. Now git!'

'Big talk for a young feller!' Ben's right

hand came up without warning and the shots took both the old man and the boy between the eyes.

Tom, hearing the two blasts of the sixgun, spurred his horse to join the others and was just in time to see Josh roll the youth out of his way before he entered the cabin.

He came out dragging an old woman. Tom blinked. He could swear it wasn't the lithe young figure going for water to the stream but he kept his mouth shut. If she had sense, she would remain hidden.

Josh twisted the woman's arm up her back and they all heard it snap. The woman screamed and slumped against Josh's chest. Josh cursed and let her drop to the ground.

'Aw hell, she wasn't worth the effort. Just my luck not to find a nice tasty piece all ready and willin' ... well, we'll have to settle for grub.'

Ben stepped inside and was soon outside again.

'They were telling the truth. It's Starvation Ranch to be sure but there's enough sow's belly for all of us and some bread and the coffee's already brewing, so come on and get at it.'

He scarcely glanced at the sprawled figures on the veranda and ignored the moaning woman. Tom stayed behind to look the woman over and to straighten her arm which was sticking out at an unnatural angle. She opened her eyes as he wrenched back the arm. He saw she was barely conscious, the colour drained from the careworn face. She reminded him of his own grandmother, a good Christian and an upright kindly woman and he felt shame that he should be riding with these men.

'Hey, Tom, don't you want to eat?' Ben's stentorian shout rocked Tom back on his heels.

'In a minute.'

'Well, hurry it up or Josh will eat your share.' He poked his head outside the door. 'What the hell are you doing? For God's sake, leave her, she's done for anyway!'

The old woman's eyes flickered open.

Then, in a breath of a whisper she managed to gasp, 'Get them away from here before they find...' Suddenly she was choking, her lips turned blue and her eyes tipped upwards as her heart gave out.

Tom cursed. It was all his fault. He should never have told Ben about the cabin and they should now be riding hell for leather for the western lands. Now there were three more dead and if Josh got wind of a young woman somewhere around, he wouldn't be satisfied until he'd had his way with her, even if he killed her in the doing of it.

He stood upright, his big shoulders slumped wearily. He had to eat, if only to keep his strength. He strode inside the small cabin, which smelled of cooking and of folks close living together and now it smelled of blood and fear.

He ate on a bench beside a small fire, his nerves a'twitch because of wondering about the girl. Where would she be? Inside the small cabin or outside in the barn or in some unknown cave? He ate and drank coffee and felt his strength return and also his courage.

Full and replete, the others lay with their boots towards the warmth, lazing and half asleep. Tom stretched. He too was being overcome by the need to relax, but his eyes examined the floor for a telltale trapdoor or signs that there was more than just logs for the roof.

But the cabin was simply built with no extras. It was just a place to eat and sleep. Tom got up, muttering he had to go relieve himself. The others barely registered his leaving. He would take a look around.

The barn held horse feed which was good. It meant their horses could stock up. He fed their own animals, a good excuse to be outside. Then he took a bucket to the stream and it was there he found her.

She was crouching low in a small jutting cave and it was her skirt that gave her away. It was snagged on a sliver of rock and he saw the movement as she tugged it free.

He was on her before she could scream,

his hand firmly across her mouth. She fought him like a tigress until he did the simple thing. He knocked her out with a slight tap to the chin, just enough to quieten her and give her a headache.

He held her in his arms until she came round. The softness of her and her smell, did strange things to him. It had been years since he'd held a woman close. He examined her features, liking what he saw, the neat little nose and the firm chin and the well-rounded mouth and the long, rich brown hair. He wondered what colour her eyes would be. They were blue when she finally opened them and turned dark with fear when she looked up at him.

'What do you want?' she whispered, and he could feel her heart flutter like a bird's wings.

'Don't be frightened. I'm not going to hurt you.'

'Who are you? Why are you here?'

Tom considered. How much to tell her. How much to leave out? He decided on as little information as possible.

'I'm Tom, and we're only passing through.'

'I heard shots and Pa always told me to make for this cave if strangers came and there was fighting. What's happened?'

'I'm sorry.' He sighed. 'Your folks are dead…'

She struggled and started to scream.

'For God's sake, keep quiet. What in hell do you think I'm doing here if I'm not trying to protect you? You've got to stay here until we go away. You understand that?'

She looked at him with troubled eyes.

'They're all dead? Grandpa and Grandma and Jesse?'

'Yeh, and you will be too if they find you, but before that one of them at least, will rape you and you're old enough to know what that means!'

She gulped. 'And you're one of them?'

'I ride with them, but I'm not one of them. It's just circumstances and the fact we rode together during the war that keeps me with them.'

'You look good and kind. Will you stay here with me until my pa returns from town?' Her lips trembled and she was beginning to realize the reality of everything. She began to shake.

He slapped her and she looked frightened. 'I'm neither good nor kind. Remember that.' His voice was brusque. 'It would be as well to remember that I cannot help you if you're foolish enough to be caught. Understand?' And he shook her roughly.

'But I've no food, only the water from the stream, and there's animals at night...' Her voice trailed away. He hardened his heart to her distress, telling himself it was for her own good.

'There's no food in the cabin,' he said callously. 'We've eaten everything, even your grandma's preserves, so don't get ideas about raiding the place during the night.'

'But how long will you be here?'

'Not long. Find somewhere where you can hide and watch, and wait until you see us move out and then wait awhile before you return. Understood?'

She nodded and he loosed her and stood up. He stood looking down at her. She was a pretty picture in her checked blue gingham with her hair drawn back in two plaits.

He turned to go and then paused.

'What's your name?'

'Rosie, Rosie Swindon.'

'How old are you, Rosie?'

'Seventeen, going on eighteen.'

'Well, good luck. You're gonna need it!'

'Will I see you again?'

He shrugged. 'You never know. Mebbe. It's a queer old world.'

She smiled shyly.

'I hope I see you again. You say you're not good or kind. I think you're lying.'

'Don't get hung up on that, Rosie Swindon. I've been a right bastard in my time, but I don't go for senseless killing or the ravishing of young girls!'

With that, he turned and walked along the stream, and he was struggling with long-suppressed desires. He could understand Josh Kirby's uncontrolled urges. He was feeling like an animal himself.

It was hard work putting the girl out of his mind. He should have stayed and bathed in the stream which might have shocked all carnal desires out of him. He set his jaw.

Ben looked up when he returned. The fire was out and Grizzly was draining the blackened coffee pot into a tin mug. Grizzly offered him the mug.

'Here, have this, it's the last. We've all had some.' Tom took it. It was lukewarm but acceptable. He took his time in drinking. He had the idea that this was going to be showdown time.

He put down the empty mug and spread his legs, his body hunched slightly forward.

'Ben, we're moving out, pronto!'

'Eh?' Ben came to his feet sharply, all semblance of sleep gone from his narrowed eyes. 'What the hell...?'

'Like I said, we're moving out!'

'Are you ... telling ... me?' He made a

move towards his gun but Tom was ready for him and the hammer clicked significantly as he thrust his own weapon forward. Suddenly Ben was wary. 'Now, take it easy, Tom, and let's talk about it. Why move out now?'

'Look, I know it sounds as if I want to take over. I don't. I only want us to leave right now.'

Ben eyed him narrowly while Josh, who'd been overcome by surprise, got his wits back. Grizzly moved back into the shadows.

'He's lying, Ben,' Josh yelled. 'Don't listen to the bastard for he must have something up his sleeve!'

'Shurrup, Josh,' Ben said, not taking his eyes off Tom. 'I'm not sure of you, Tom. Why should we leave right now? What did you see out there when you were snooping around?'

'Nothing but what you could see if you moved your arse outside. It's a dead-end place and I've got a feeling that it's jinxed.'

Josh laughed.

'That sixth sense you get from your Indian squaw grandma working overtime, is it?' He was too slow to dodge the uppercut Tom threw at him. It stung but didn't do much damage to his jaw but a lot to his pride. It was another black mark against Tom.

Tom's eyes slid from Josh to Ben. He took little notice of Grizzly.

'Look, I'm only asking for us to move out.'

'Why, Tom?'

'Because we'll soon have another posse on our trail and if we ever want to reach Kansas, we must get riding, and I don't want my neck stretching. Good enough?'

Ben smiled with his lips but his eyes remained hard and suspicious.

'Fair enough, Tom. We'll leave it at that. I'll just take me a look around while you fellers see to the horses, and you Josh, I want no quarrelling. Keep that big mouth of yours shut!'

Tom watched him move out, his stomach tight. If Rosie was as smart as he hoped, she would keep out of sight. Still...

His stomach still knotted, he did what he had to do and, when Ben returned satisfied that there was nothing worth taking, he turned his back on Ben to hide his relief and forked his horse ready to ride.

Ben looked up at him.

'I still can't figure why you were in such a goldarn hurry. We could have slept easy...'

'What? In that infested pigsty? You must be joking!'

'It did smell a bit but the fleas pestered me none.' He scratched his head. 'Still, they might have by morning.' He looked about him. 'You know, this is a mighty nice place. I might come back here some day...'

'Look, let's not waste time messing about. I have a feeling. Let's be away!' Tom glowered at Ben.

'Y'know, I'm beginning to think you've got some of your Blackfoot grandma's medicine in you, bud! Somethin's buggin' you. You're like an ant on a fire-stick!'

'Look, just quit the witticisms and let's be away!'

'All right … all right, we're ready, so let's go!'

They rode away, Ben and Josh leading and Grizzly and Tom a little behind. Tom felt a great relief, far more than he should have done. It would have been a pity if that pretty young thing had been ravished by a murderous brute like Josh.

They slowed to a walk as they reached the top of the trail and it was when Ben and Josh reached the gap that Tom paused.

'You ride on, Grizzly, and I'll catch up. I think my horse's got a stone in her shoe.'

Grizzly nodded and rode on and Tom dismounted and faced the valley. His sentiments were the same as Ben's. This place could be made into a wonderful home for a man with ambition, who wanted to settle down with a good woman and raise a family.

Suddenly there was a gnawing ache in him which was half physical and mixed with something in his mind. He thought of Rosie walking to the stream for water and he thought of her softness. God, he was being a fool, and an old fool at that. He was nearly twenty years older than she was. Anyhow, he would never be back. By the way things were shaping up, he'd be dead, if those two fools had their way.

His eyes narrowed. He was sure he could see a smidgeon of blue and it was moving, a tiny speck to be sure, if it wasn't just his imagination.

He mounted up and then faced down the valley and on impulse, he took off his bandanna and waved it above his head.

Then he was laughing for a fluttering white handkerchief waved back.

Suddenly he was filled with hope and energy. By God, he would see this place again, or die in the attempt!

He raked his horse's ribs and he was galloping through the gap in the hills and, far ahead, he could see the mad gallop of what he had come to call the devil's spawn.

FOUR

Over the next six months, they rode forever westward, raiding and pillaging to survive. It was easy to come upon some lonely farmstead or cabin unawares and shoot up the occupants and then in a frenzy of glee and anticipation paw through their belongings and eat their food in comfort.

Sometimes Ben and Josh got lucky and there was a woman to ease their frustrations. He and Grizzly would listen to the screams until Grizzly would walk away, head down, and find comfort in his pipe as far away from the homestead as possible.

Twice Tom had tried to intervene, but one of the brothers stood guard while the other enjoyed himself. The second time, Ben shot at him between the legs and grimly threatened that the next time he intervened, he'd shoot for real and he'd lose his balls.

It was in a small town called Benson Falls that they nearly caught it. They'd raided a ranch a day's ride away, and they'd all bathed and shaved and got a change of clothes. They were drunk with success, and several bottles of good whiskey, soaking up the good stew that an old Mexican woman was tending in the cookhouse.

They were confident, piss-proud and reckless enough to try something new.

'How's about going into the next town we come across instead of cutting around it, and trying out the local females?' Josh asked as he tipped down his throat the last of the whiskey in his bottle.

Ben laughed, his usual heavy caution dulled by food and liquor.

'Why not? Nobody will recognize us and we've got the money. We've all got rolls in our pockets to spend as we like. What about it you two? Are you game?'

Grizzly spat on the ground and rubbed his hands together.

'I'm not so much bothered by the women but I'd sure like a hand or two of poker. It would be like the old days.' He sounded a little wistful.

'What about you, Tom? You're the one who's usually doin' the preachin'. Would it put a smile on that goldarn sour face of yours?'

Tom shrugged. He knew that Josh was about at exploding point. He was always quieter and more amenable to reason after he'd slaked his passions on some unfortunate woman. The trouble with Josh was that a frightened woman turned him on. Tom wasn't too sure about the effects of a local whore. Josh might have to do something drastic to frighten a whore, and for that, a whole town might go mad. You could rob banks and hold up stagecoaches, and only those who were actually robbed would care a hoot, but molest one of their whores, and every man jack took it personal.

'It's a risk, but as you say, we'll not be recognized, as long as Josh here doesn't do anything outrageous.'

'Wha'd'ya mean?' Josh fired back, his eyes glassy and furious. 'You're always pokin' and diggin' at me. I don't like it. One of these days you and me are goin' to have a showdown.'

'Shurrup, Josh, we all know what a fool you can be,' Ben cut in, 'and it's only Tom who has the guts to say anythin'. You've caused more grief than any of us, through your lust for women. He's only sayin' you gotta be careful. No stickin' a knife at a girl's throat to make her scream as you're screwin' her! None of your funny tricks! Right!'

Josh nodded, his face sullen. He threw the empty bottle across the room and it smashed against the log wall.

'When do we ride?'

'We'll have a good night's kip here, and ride at dawn.'

'What about the old woman?'

Ben laughed. 'I think we'll leave our preacher friend to dispose of her. He needs the practice. 'Wha'd'ya say, Tom?'

Tom gritted his teeth and glared at Ben.

'I don't need any practice at killin', Ben. I did enough of it during the war.'

'Aye, all in the name of the Confederacy and all in hot blood, but you've been mighty slow in doin' some actual butcherin' in cold blood. Let's see you do it now, buddy boy.'

Tom gave him a long look and then heaved himself upright. One of these days it would give him pleasure to take Ben in cold blood.

'Seein' you're the boss, I'll do it.' And he walked outside and across the yard to the cookhouse. He stepped inside and saw the Mexican woman crouched down beside her fire. She was still groggy from the horrendous blow Josh had given her on arrival. Her face was swollen and her eyes puffed up so that she was nearly blind.

He knew that she realized what had happened to her boss and his son as she looked at him. He put out a hand to her.

'Don't be afraid. I'm not going to kill you. Just scream.' He grabbed part of a cut-up liver and lunged at her. She screamed instinctively as he screwed the liver in her face. Blood dripped from it down her front and, taking his Colt, he fired a shot into the wall behind her, and then another.

She slumped with shock.

'Lie still,' he commanded sharply. 'You're dead!'

He paused long enough to wipe away the blood from his hand and then returned to the house. Ben looked up at him, noting the tension in the face.

'So you did it?'

Tom only nodded and hunkered down by the fire.

Ben nodded at Grizzly, who went out to investigate. Tom's nerves knotted. He hoped the old woman was smart. She was.

Grizzly came back and nodded to Ben.

'Good. Now let's get some rest and be out of here by dawn.'

Josh was hung-over next morning but cheered a little when he found the rancher's black stetson emblazoned with silver conches. He jammed it on his head.

'How do I look?'

'As good as you'll ever look.' Ben's reply was surly. He wasn't in a good mood. The two men lying dead just outside the door were beginning to affect his stomach. He never could abide bad smells.

'It fits well. I'm going to have it.' He led the way jauntily as they left. Then he turned in the saddle and looked back.

'Shouldn't we fire the place?'

'Use your brains,' snapped Ben. 'A fire would show for miles. With a bit of luck it could be days or weeks before anyone comes a'callin'.'

They followed the trail from the ranch and it hit a main highway, and leisurely took their time and finally came to a wooden sign which read Benson Falls in crooked letters.

They rode in three abreast along a wide crooked street with shacks on either side, some tin-roofed, others with false fronts. They passed a horse-feed store and livery stable, a store with tin baths and brushes hanging outside and a narrow cabin which had a doctor's shingle outside.

Then they came to the saloon and they all paused, looking up at the sign, The Golden Steer, and Josh gave a rebel yell, which made the townsfolk pause and stare.

Then Josh was down off his horse, whipping reins over the rail out front and up the veranda steps as if he had a fire up his arse. The others followed more slowly.

Josh was already bellying up to the bar and the thin, miserable bartender was laying out four shot glasses and a bottle.

Josh grinned, for once forgetting his animosity to Tom.

'Come on, fellers, get at it and let's get in the mood.' He drank his first drink down in one gulp and poured another and sighed with pleasure.

Grizzly's eyes lighted up when he spied a card school in a far corner. He sauntered across to watch, waiting to see if one of the players would pack up. He was in luck as a bored looking man looked up at him.

'You wanna play, bud? I'm nearly broke. You could save me a lot of grief.'

Grizzly grinned. 'I'll play.' He sat down when the other man heaved himself clear.

Tom looked about him, enjoying the smell of liquor and humanity. This was as it should be and it was incredible how he'd missed all this normal fraternizing without having to look behind him. He glanced at the man next to him.

'Kinda quiet, isn't it, round here?'

The man laughed. 'You want to be here on a Saturday night when the cowpokes come thundering in. They set the place alight.'

'Oh? You get many outsiders comin' in?'

'Enough. All good for trade. They spend well. I'm the local blacksmith. I do a good job on a horse if you've travelled far.'

Tom looked at the bulk of the man and then at his big round face.

'I bet you do. I know a man who's proud of his job when I see one. I might just take you up on that.'

The man visibly swelled with pride.

'Here, have a snort on me, bud!'

Tom smiled and took the proffered drink. He sighed with satisfaction.

'You got a good town here. Seems thriving'.'

'Uhuh. Most of the business comes from the ranches. We're a bit way out for the railroad and the big herds but we do OK.

'Nothing much happens in these parts but it's a livin' and we don't get bothered none with the Indians now they're on their own lands.'

'What about owlhoots?'

The big man laughed and a bunch of cowboys coming in at that moment looked to see what all the fun was about.

'Hey, Charlie! We was lookin' for you to fix our hosses.' A tall red-haired cowboy strode across with the rolling gait of a man with bow legs.

'Hiya, Luke, meet...' He looked at Tom. 'Damn me, I don't even know your name.' Tom smiled and thrust out a hand to the newcomer.

'Tom … Tom Hitchens, but everyone calls me Tom.'

'Hiya, Tom. I'm Luke Short, ramrod of the Circle Y and these are my boys. Where you heading, buddy?'

'Oh, just moseying along.'

'Travelling alone?'

Tom nodded to Grizzly, already deep in a game.

'No, I got buddies I trail along with.' He glanced about him for Ben and Josh and just saw the pair of them following two women upstairs. Their gaudy blue and red gowns grimy, their faces hard and lined, the thought went through Tom that one of them was old enough to be Josh's mother. A fleeting memory of Rosie's sweet fresh face distracted him for a moment and then he was listening again to Luke.

'What about it then? We could do with a couple of extra men seeing how Jake broke his ankle brandin' a calf and Bill took a header down a cliff astride a maverick hoss.'

'Eh? Oh, a job? Well now, I think not.

We're aimin' to ride on into Texas...'

Luke gave a belly laugh. 'You're goin' to have corns on your arses before you get there. Do you realize how far it is?'

Tom looked around at the grinning cowboys, even Charlie joined in.

'So what? Don't any of you want to ride over the next hill and see what lies ahead?'

'Aw, you've got ants in your pants. We be settled here. It's quiet and we get no trouble. We're off the track when it comes to outlaws and hard men. There's nothin' to attract 'em. Even the bank doesn't hold much. Yeh, we're a sober enough town, except mebbe on a Saturday night when some of the boys live it up. That's how we like it.'

Luke spoke with self-satisfied confidence. Tom wondered how he would react if he told him he was one of the Kirby gang. He would probably shit his pants.

'How about you boys havin' a drink on me?'

An hour later, Tom was more than a little drunk, reckless in fact, and those inhibitions he was usually riddled with were gone like mist in the sun. He drank happily.

Then Josh followed by Ben came down the stairs and Josh, taking a look at Tom and the crowd drinking with him, hollered, 'Hi, Tom, introduce me to your friends!' And with a cocky rolling gait walked across the room, jamming his hat at a jaunty angle, and grinning. 'Hi, everybody!'

Luke stared at him and frowned and then turned to Tom.

'You know this punk?'

'Yeh, he's one of the buddies I ride with. Why?' Suddenly fingers of ice were crawling up Tom's spine.

'Because he's wearing Bert Hamilton's stetson with all those conches Bert's proud of. What's he doin' with Bert's hat, buddy?' Luke's voice had grown cold and suddenly there was a silence you could have cut with a crosscut saw.

A pause, broken by Grizzly leaping up from the table gun out and, as the bunch of cowboys gaped, Ben and Josh exploded into action. Their bullets followed in quick succession and everyone was diving for cover. Tom sent a slug into the ceiling and lit for the batwings which swung wildly as he catapulted through.

He wanted no part of any massacre. They were a good set of drinking mates and he cursed Josh for wanting that damned hat. Everyone had his own personal hat on which he put his mark. The fool should have known that someone might recognize it.

Then he was helping old Grizzly aboard and when Ben and Josh hurtled out of the batwings he sent a couple of warning slugs high up just to hold the rabble back.

The horses reared. There were screams from passers-by who scattered and then they were thundering down the straggly street with the occasional bullet gouging dust around them.

Josh was laughing wildly and when they were on the edge of town, he took off the offending stetson and waved it with insulting abandonment at the men who were now pouring out of the saloon.

Their headlong gallop took them further south-west, but it was in Benson Falls that the mischief had been done. There were posters following them and it was when they rode through a small cattle town that Josh first caught sight of the bad likeness, drawn by a poor artist, on a poster outside the sheriff's office.

'Just look at that! Hell, I've half a mind to complain and sue for bad exposure!' They drew close, horses stamping as they gazed down at the posters. 'Mind you, they're a bit mean on the ree-ward, don't you think? A measly hundred dollars each. It ain't fair!'

Josh was disgusted. Ben was irritable.

'For God's sake stop actin' like a damned kid! Don't you realize it's serious? We've come all this way and they're right behind us!'

Josh's face was a study. 'How can they be? We left that posse miles back...'

'Jesus! They're right behind us because of the telegraph; it doesn't have to be the same posse, dope!'

'Stop callin' me, Ben, or I'm goin' to get mad and you know what that means! Now looka here…'

'No. You look here and listen good. There's goin' to be no more rape and no more shootin' at the blink of an eye. We're gonna travel respectable. We've got cash and we pay our way and we keep our heads down until we come to Texas. Right?'

'Aw, Ben, Texas is a long way aways. We gotta have excitement and women, at least I have. Life's not worth livin' otherwise.'

Ben sighed and Tom and Grizzly kept silent. They all knew that Josh was the weak link who could put them all on the gallows tree.

'I'm warnin' you, Josh: I'll put a bullet in you myself if you put a foot wrong.'

The two brothers glared at each other.

'You really wouldn't do that, your own kid brother?'

'Try me.' They glared some more until Tom coughed and broke the tension.

'Look, it's no good fightin'. We gotta keep our heads down. Ben's right. We cut across country and make for Abilene.'

'Why Abilene?'

'Must we keep having to spell it out? That's where they take the cattle that's been rounded up! Where the trail herds are, there's the gold and dollars and the opportunities. You're like a blasted kid! You'd never survive without us, Josh. I wish you'd keep your feet on the ground, boy!'

Josh glared at Tom. 'Are you going to let Tom get away with that, Ben?'

'He's right, Josh. You are a big kid with your brains between your legs! I think that zonk on the head did something to you, boy. You've been crazy ever since it happened. You've gotta control yourself or else you're goin' to do us all in. Savvy?'

'Why you...' Josh's Colt came up but Tom leaned over and knocked it out of his fist and all the horses started to fidget at the fracas.

'Steady,' growled Grizzly, 'or else those

folk down there are gonna know we're comin' in!'

Ben leaned over and dragged on Josh's reins as he was about to rowel his horse in temper.

'Josh! Control yourself or by God, I'll plug you!' And, as his horse danced and bucked, he brought his arm round and his fist caught Josh across the face.

Josh crashed to the ground, whimpering, and Ben's lips curled.

'He's piss-proud when he's got an itch to scratch, but he's just a load of shit a dung beetle wouldn't eat off, when it boils down to it. For God's sake, you jelly-bag, just quit squawking and mount up and do as you're told for once!' He looked at Tom. 'That idea's good. We'll quit the main trails and ride south-west. We'll avoid the towns and we'll travel as cattle drovers lookin' for business. We got dough, so there's no need to advertise ourselves and we'll all stop thinkin' about women. Did you hear that, Josh?'

'Yeh,' came the sulky reply, 'but it'll not

take the itch away none.'

'A scrape with a rough stone will help that itch, Josh. Just holler and we'll help you out some!' Grizzly's belly laugh didn't improve Josh's mood and, as they prepared to ride down into the valley, he followed, his eyes on Tom's back. What he wouldn't have given for a chance to stick a knife in it at this moment.

FIVE

They walked their horses slowly and cautiously in full view of the cabin and then stopped well back from rifle range.

'Ho, the house,' Ben's stentorian voice echoed around the enclosing hills. He called again when he got no reply. 'Ho, the house. Anyone at home?'

Another five minutes passed and Ben signalled for them to move ahead. Two steps forward and the sunbaked door opened and a man stepped outside holding an army rifle. It pointed at Ben's middle with surprising firmness.

'Don't take another step, mister, or you get it in spite of those bastards behind you. Now, who are you and what do you want?'

'We want to trade horses. We can pay good money.'

The man looked at them with suspicion.

'You don't look like horse-traders, none that I know and I know 'em all within a two-hundred mile radius.'

Ben tried conciliation.

'We heard of your stock way back and, as we deal in the best, here we are.' He smiled and spread his hands.

'I think you're lying. Pedigree horse-traders don't ride half-dead nags like yours. Yours are not even groomed, so split the breeze, fellers or I'll give you a taste of what I'm good at!'

'Sir, we've come a long way...'

'Like hell you have! And I don't care if

you've come from the President himself, you'll not get my stock!' And with that he aimed the rifle above Ben's head and fired. Ben's hat flew off and fluttered to the ground as all the horses pranced and nickered in alarm.

'You're making a big mistake,' bawled Ben and he dismounted to retrieve his hat. He looked ruefully at it and put a finger through a hole in the crown. 'I see you've been a military man. It takes one to know one.'

The rifle was lowered.

'You were in the army?'

'Yep. All the way through. Saw action in the Battle of the Big River Bridge and at Brice's Crossroads and at Vicksburg to name just a few encounters.'

'You were lucky to come out alive. I take it you were a bluecoat and these men were with you?'

Ben laughed. 'Yeh, we're old buddies. We trust each other and in these hard times we stick together. Any harm in that?'

The man shrugged.

'Not as long as you are what you claim. You can come in and eat but I'm not doing business with you. Understood?'

'But...'

'Look, mister, you can eat if you like but if you don't, then it's no skin off my nose. You can git. I've got half-a-dozen army rifles as well as this beauty and they're all trained on you right this minute. So, do you want to eat or not?'

Ben aired all their views with his succinct, 'We'll eat.'

They were allowed to water their horses and one of the men coming from the barn at the old man's whistle showed them where to find fodder. He was sullen but he sure knew how to use the Spencer rifle and Tom noted it was clean and oiled as if for instant use.

He also noted that the men when they came out of their well-thought-out hidey-holes acted like military men still on duty.

He was eating a second helping of pumpkin pie, served by a quiet, faded woman in well-patched gingham when he voiced the thought which sprang to mind.

'You get a lot of aggravation, sir? I see your men act in a trained military fashion.'

'We get some smart arses every now and again who think they can rustle my stock. We have our own way of dealing with them. It's enough to say that we've never lost our stock to rustlers yet!'

'Oh! And just how do you foil 'em, Mr, er...'

'Brockenridge. Captain James Brockenridge, late of General Grant's own Northern Command Rifles!' There was great pride in the man; he puffed out like some pouter pigeon.

Suddenly, Josh was on his feet and the mug in his hand crashed down on the table, breaking, and home-made beer spilled everywhere.

'What the hell...?' Brockenridge stared, shocked and momentarily paralysed as were the others except for Ben who rose seconds later.

'*You! It was you and your men who killed our folks!*' Josh clawed at his gun.

'But you're Yankees…'

'Like hell we are!'

Then everything happened at once. Ben's gun took one of the men from the barn. Grizzly's gun spat twice, missing one man and wounding another, while Josh took a shot at Brockenridge and missed and Brockenridge's handgun clicked and jammed. So he was a rifle man, Tom registered, as his own gun took a man in the throat.

A great weight descended on Tom and he went down. Instinct saved him as a bunched fist caught him on the side of the head as he rolled clear. Then he was twisting round and clawing at his assailant's eyes. He was a man as big as a house. He smelled of horse muck and iron filings. Tom reckoned he was Brockenridge's farrier.

The man got him in a bear-like grip and Tom gasped, knowing his ribs would crack soon. He gave a frenzied heave and reaching for the black iron pan which had held the stew, swung it hard and connected with the man's head. A brown gooey mess slopped over the man's face. It was still hot and the man screamed and scrambled away on his knees.

Tom held on to the pan with its trivet handle and soon he had a small space around him. He paused for breath and to take stock of what was happening. Josh was bleeding but grinning as he scooped up an inert body and threw him at Brockenridge.

Brockenridge ducked and the man crashed against the wall. Then suddenly it was all over. Ben was staggering and breathing heavily and holding his side. Josh was dragging Brockenridge up to a sitting position and shaking him like a terrier with a rat.

'You bastard! We're goin' to swing you up for what you did, you foul, maggot-infested lump of shit! You and the damn lot of you! But before that...' His mad eyes cast around and he saw the woman crouched in a corner behind a rough wooden blanket box. Josh gave a chilling laugh. 'We'll do what you and your men did. Do you remember the cabin and the folks of Gaby's Drift? The woman and her daughter who were raped repeatedly after you stripped them and made them dance? Well, see that woman over there? She's going to do exactly as them.'

He lunged across the room and dragged the petrified woman out of the corner by her hair. Then he took her wrists in one hand and tore her dress down to the waist. It was then she was galvanized back to life. She screamed and struggled and he lost his hold on one of her wrists and she raked his face with her nails.

It all happened so fast that Ben and Tom just stood and stared. Then Tom was battling his way between them, taking blows on his back and shoulders from both.

'Get out of the damned way!' shouted Josh. 'I'll make this bitch pay!'

'Are you quite mad?' yelled Tom. 'It's

nothing to do with her!'

'Now to hell with that, preacher man. It's an eye for an eye!'

Tom breathed heavily and then put all his strength into the blow which felled Josh. He lay still and Tom took the weight of the woman.

'It's all right. Get yourself into the other room and stay there.' She went.

Ben passed a shaken hand over his forehead.

'Thanks, Tom. I nearly went along with Josh.'

Josh groaned and stirred. 'What ... what happened?'

'Tom stopped you from violating that woman.'

'And you let him? They were your folks as well as mine. I saw it all. You didn't.'

Ben's mouth quivered and then steeled itself.

'There's been enough acting like animals. You torture that woman and you make yourself as low as him. Do you want that?'

'Hell, we've done plenty we can't boast about!'

'Yeh, we're devils on horseback and as long as we live, we'll always be the same.' Ben sighed. 'We're a doomed breed, Josh, all of us. It's got to us. We don't know right from wrong.'

'Hell, you sound like Tom here. I thought he was the only one who'd gone soft. What we goin' to do with him, Ben?' He pointed his thumb in the direction of Brockenridge who was half-sitting, half-lying on the floor, his left leg stuck out at an angle.

It sounded like a challenge. Tom waited anxiously for Ben's reply. Did Ben realize the kid was challenging his leadership and perhaps the respect which had always held Josh in check?

The answer was crucial. Contempt was something that was never erased. It was make-or-break time with Josh.

Ben paused only a moment and then he said softly but with deadly menace, 'We hang 'em high and we do it now. Satisfied?'

'What about amusing ourselves with 'em first?'

'We were soldiers, not Indians. We hang 'em. That's it.'

Josh nodded, but Tom didn't like the look in Josh's eyes. Ben as well as he would have to sleep light of nights...

Tom looked around. 'Where's Grizzly?' They found him under the big blacksmith. His neck was broken, but the smith was dead too, with a knife through his heart.

Tom felt regret. He was going to miss the near-silent old man. They'd been through a lot together and he could always be relied on. There was also another reason to miss him. There had been a tacit understanding between them that they should watch each other's back. It was going to be harder watching Josh.

The barn was cleared and lunging reins slung over the main rafter and soon Brockenridge and what remained of his men were slung up. Brockenridge gritted his teeth when it was his turn.

'You'll pay for this outrage. I've men out on the range who'll come after you.'

'But you won't know, will you, my old cock?' Josh wielded the knife and blood spurted from between Brockenridge's legs as he was dragged high by Ben and Tom, to swing and kick.

They waited until all were still. Then Ben stirred.

'We'd best be away before the men return. We'll pick out two horses each and ride nonstop.'

'What about Grizzly?'

'We'll take him with us on the back of one of the horses and we'll bury him on the trail.'

Tom nodded. 'And the woman? We'll leave her fastened in the back room?'

Ben nodded and looked at Josh who turned away.

'Yeh, we'll leave the woman,' Ben mumbled.

But when they rode away, Ben thrust his extra horse's reins into Tom's hands.

'Hold this. I forgot something.' He galloped back to the cabin.

Josh laughed as if pleased.

'What's he forgot?'

'What do *you* think?'

Then the shot came and it echoed around the hills, becoming quieter and quieter until there was just a whisper and Ben rode back and took the reins without a word or a glance at Tom.

'You killed her.'

Ben gave Tom a look of pure dislike.

'I had to. You know that. A good general never leaves witnesses.'

'We're not fighting a war now, Ben.'

'Is that what you think? Well, let me tell you something, buddy boy, we're fighting a damned harder war than the last. We have to, to survive. You and I and Josh here have no future. We've got to fight dirty to live! Or have you gone too soft to see this?'

'I've still got dreams for the future, Ben. Some day…'

'Oh, shurrup, you make me sick! You're

just as crazy as Josh here, and I'll tell you now, I couldn't care less about the woman. She's just another statistic as General Robert E. Lee would say. Now let's ride!'

He set off at a gallop and Josh gave the rebel yell and raked his horse's ribs, his second mount thundering behind. Tom followed at a slower pace, keeping the brothers in sight. His heart was heavy. Was Ben right? Had they changed, never to be really human again? Things that looked like men but with no real human feelings?

Horror laid icy fingers on his heart. Wouldn't it have been better to die for the Cause, then become an automaton, who battled to live and eat just to get through another day?

He thought of the fresh-faced Rosie. If he ever saw her again how would she react if she knew that the real core of him was dead?

There was no choice. He had to go on, to what end he didn't know. Maybe it was to protect Ben and Josh from themselves. Maybe it was to protect someone else. Yet that couldn't be so for he'd made a damned bad job of helping that woman lying back there. His thoughts whirled as his mount lengthened his stride, the spare horse keeping pace for it was a stable companion.

It was the best ride he'd had in years. These pedigree horses had grace and style, not like the broken-down cavalry horses or the wild mustangs. Against all reason he found his mood change subtly. It wasn't all doom and gloom.

The wind against his face exhilarated him. He watched Ben and Josh in the distance, horses bunched and one of them carrying poor old Grizzly. Well, he was out of the rat race now and he wished him well. They would bury him at their first stopping place.

He bent low over the horse's neck and dug in his heels. The horse responded. It was like riding a race with the spare horse pounding behind. He was still capable of emotion. He wasn't dead yet. Maybe Ben was wrong, only time would show.

SIX

They were skylined. Bunched in a group. They looked down at a sprawling crossroads way-station. There was also a store and several renegade Indians lounged about waiting for free whiskey.

There was also a stage coach, all ready for off, horses dancing friskily and the driver using all his muscle to stop the horses hightailing for the trail.

There were two women climbing aboard, and what looked like a drummer, and a preacher man. Josh whistled.

'Look at those women! I fancy the pretty one in blue. I wouldn't mind bein' either a travellin' salesman or a preacher for a day! Yes, sir!'

'Shurrup, Josh! Don't get your mind fixed on what you can't have. Look at them horses down there in the corral. Pick out the likeliest. At least you know a good horse when you see one.'

Josh laughed.

'We was sure bugged when we took these nags. All show and no stamina.' And he looked with distaste at the horses still remaining with them.

It had been a long haul and though the breed horses were a good ride, they didn't match the mustangs for stamina. They were good for a quick burst of speed, but they were used to plenty of grooming and balanced feed and they'd suffered greatly during the last few months.

They'd planted Grizzly just as soon as they were out of danger of any would-be posse. They had watched their backs but there were no telltale signs of being followed. No campfires, no suspicious clouds of dust during daylight hours. Nothing.

'Seems strange ridin' with a feller and eatin' and drinkin' with him for years and not knowin' one damn thing about him,'

Josh said thoughtfully during one of his better moods. 'Did you know where he came from, Ben?'

Ben shook his head. 'He was never a talkative man. I met him first, ridin' with Quantrill. I think he came from his neck of the woods. Did he ever talk to you, Tom?'

'Nope, and I didn't ask. A man's got a right to keep himself to himself. Maybe he was runnin' away from something or someone. We'll never know now.'

'Yeh, we sure miss the old bastard,' and Ben laughed. And that had been that.

Now Tom rubbed a roughened hand over his whiskers. He itched and he had travel sores on his arse. He needed a bath. He also needed a damn big steak to put the taste of snakemeat out of his mouth. And he needed a drink.

'Well, what shall we do? Gamble on it and go down there when the stage moves on and get us some decent food and trade in these horses and maybe get cleaned up and buy us some new clothes?' Tom looked at Josh consideringly. 'How's about you? Can you act like a law-abidin' cowboy for a few hours?'

'If you don't get me riled none, beforehand. I don't quite like you doubtin' me, Tom.'

'Oh, hell! No offence, Josh. I just wanted to know!'

'You shouldn't have had to ask!'

'I know, and whose fault's that?'

The situation was heating up.

'Steady on, you two. Josh will stick with me. Right? Now we go in and we first go for clothes to the store and then we go and have us a bath...'

'Couldn't we have a drink first?'

'No, Josh. We eat and drink afterwards and then you and I shall dicker over the horses while Tom here gets us some supplies. Right?'

Tom nodded. 'Sounds good. Then we ride out like regular cowboys lookin' for work.'

'Yeh, and if we keep our eyes and ears open we might just get ourselves jobs and merge into the countryside, so to speak.'

'You mean we'll have to really work?' Josh sounded horrified. Tom's lips twitched. It would do the kid good to have to give way to a little discipline.

'Not for long, Josh. Just long enough to cast around and see what offers. We're getting' near the big cattle trails and if we keep our noses clean, then we might do a big snatch later on. Right?'

Josh sighed with relief. 'For one minute, Ben, I thought you was goin' soft. I couldn't stand a quiet life. You know that, don't you, Ben?'

Ben sighed. 'Yeh, I know that.'

'Ben?'

'Yeh?'

'You would never turn a gun on me, would you, Ben?'

Ben hesitated. Then, 'No Josh. I guess I couldn't do it.'

'I'm glad, Ben, because I'd hate to have to shoot you too. You know somethin' Ben, I couldn't do without you. If you ever copped it, it would be like ridin' a horse both blind and deaf. I wouldn't know what to do first!'

'Josh, nothing's goin' to happen to me, so forget it. Just act nice and calm and we'll start goin' down there nice and easy and we'll get us some grub and we'll have a drink and then we'll see what's what. Right?'

Josh nodded and they started to pick their way down the narrow trail.

Thoughtfully Tom followed behind.

The stagecoach was leaving before they hit the main trail and somehow the atmosphere had changed. Once again it was a sleepy community and the Indians had gone back to where they'd come from when the stagecoach appeared. All was quiet.

They were watched as they trotted directly to the store, dismounting with deliberate slowness and hitching the horses to the rail.

At once several idlers moved nearer to examine the horses.

'Nice horses, mister, but you've rode 'em too far to do 'em any good,' an old-timer said to Ben.

'What's it to you, old man?' Ben's tone was a mite terse. The old man raised white eyebrows.

'Nothin', mister. But I don't like to see good horse-flesh abused. No sir!'

Tom listened silently. It would be a good job when they shucked the five horses they had left. One had just lain down and died after they travelled over the sierras.

The storekeeper was waiting when they moved inside.

'Well, gents, what can I do for you?'

'Can we get baths in these parts?'

'Yeh. The way-station is hotel and bath-house and brothel as well if you want women. I suppose you do want women, when you wants a bath and the like?'

Josh's face brightened but Ben put a restraining hand on his arm and Josh's face turned to its usual sullen look.

'No. We're just wantin' clobber and then we'll get ourselves to the bathhouse. How's the barber? Not too cutthroat, is he?'

'Middlin', if you don't squirm and there's nothin' drastic goin' on outside. I mind once he nearly cut Hal Pierce's throat when a gun-crazy bastard let rip outside. We're pretty peaceful now the stage has gone so you're in luck.'

They chose checked shirts and canvas trousers and two sets of unbleached wool vests and long johns and Josh picked out a fancy vest, more in keeping with the black stetson with the silver conches.

Tom and Ben were more conservative. They settled for soft leather jackets and they carried the whole lot over to the way-station to find the bathhouse.

It didn't take long for the water boy to fill three baths in the cabin built behind what they found was an hotel of sorts.

It was luxury even though the sudsy water stung blisters and sores. The yellow soap smelled clean and brought back memories of his mother for Tom. He hadn't thought of her in years. He wondered what she would have thought of him now if she'd lived to know what happened to him. His mind slid away from the answer. Finally when the water was nearly cold they heaved themselves out and dried themselves on rough greyish-white towels.

They looked at each other and laughed.

'Hell! We look like three white slugs!' Josh grinned. 'I haven't seen myself for months!'

'You smell a damn sight better too.'

'And you both do. I was wonderin' what was different about you. D'ye know, I kinda miss that smell...'

They all laughed and Ben threw sudsy water over him while Tom lobbed what was left of his soap.

'Cheeky young bugger!'

Clean clothes and a shave did wonders and they stuck to their plan and went to eat. Whatever happened next, they were prepared for it. A great steak running with blood, fried potatoes and new bread and dried apple pie and enough coffee to drown in. Tom let his belt out a notch.

Then it was back to the store for Tom to

buy the stores while Josh and Ben took the horses for exchange at the station. They were prepared to dicker and two hours later came away with three rather ugly mounts, but were guaranteed stayers and would ride up and down any mountains they wanted to tackle.

Ben had also got wind of a huge cattle drive making for the railroad and if they wanted to tag along, all they had to do was find the cattle boss. He wasn't known to be a generous man but he paid going rates with feed for both horse and man thrown in. Ben winked.

'Once at the railroad, we could cash in and take a ride. What you say?'

Tom thought it a good idea. They could wait until a train came west and they could ride all the way to Abilene. They could even have their horses aboard. No sweat.

Josh wasn't so sure. It sounded like work and Josh wasn't cut out for disciplined work. He wanted the excitement of planned attack and escape with the adrenalin flowing and the sweet pounding of success hurtling through his veins. He was a child of war, not peace.

'Aw hell, Ben, must we? I don't fit in with no snotty big-headed cowpokes. You know I ain't no cattle man.'

'Then now's the time to learn, Josh. Times change and we've all gotta change too. You keep your head down, boy, and watch what them fellers do. Someday we're goin' to get us a herd of our own and we've gotta know how to handle 'em.'

'I thought we was goin' to let them palookas do the work and us just take the spondulicks?'

Ben sighed. 'Oh, Josh, how long do you think we're gonna last at that game? Down there in Texas they've got owlhoots robbin' owlhoots like they live off one another. Gunslingers are as thick as cents on the ground.'

'You mean we go soft like Tom here? Hell, Ben, what's got into you? I don't want that. I want for us to go out into them Indian territories they talk about where the gangs hole up. They say they've got wild women out there…'

'And bloody wild Indians too, Josh. Come on, boy, get real. We've gotta change!'

Josh looked at his brother with disillusionment and dislike.

'I'll go along with you now, Ben, but someday I'm gonna break away from you and go my own way.'

'Oh yeah? And pigs might fly!' Suddenly Josh was lunging at Ben arms flailing and the horses forgotten in the sudden mêlée.

Tom grabbed the reins and dragged the nervously prancing beasts clear while a crowd gathered around the two combatants. Soon, the new clothes were caked in dust as the crowd cheered and took bets as to the outcome.

Josh, his eyes glazed with maniacal fury, lashed out with more force than skill, and even though Ben dodged and weaved and parried the blows defensively, he was bleeding when Tom finally smashed Josh on the side of the head and felled him.

At once there was a ruckus from the crowd.

'That wasn't fair! You sonofabitch, you shoulda left them to it! You want stringin' up. I had a dollar on the young 'un and he looked like winnin'!' There were other more dangerous threats and Tom had to back off while Ben staggered around catching his breath.

Then, wind back, Ben gave a stentorian shout which made the watchers step back.

'Out of the way, you scumbags while I see to this crazy fool.' Ben heaved him upright and tossed him over his shoulders and stalked off, Tom following with the horses to the stable where Ben flung Josh down and kicked him in the ribs.

'Wake up, you damned pesky bastard, we're gonna ride whether you're fit or not.'

Josh groaned and raised his head and then flopped it again.

'My head … what happened?'

'Tom slapped you down. Now get up and

stick your head in that there horse trough and quick about it.'

Mumbling under his breath, Josh staggered upright and did what he was told, water sloshing all ways ruining the effect of his new duds.

'I'm ready. What now?'

'We ride as soon as Tom picks up the dry goods. You stacked up on plenty of shells, Tom?'

'Yeh, no sweat. I got enough for an army.'

'Good. When will they be ready?'

'In an hour. Everything's being packed on a mule.'

'So we can ride independent if we don't like the prospect of working with others?' Ben gave Josh a long darkling glance as if daring him to make a comment.

'Yep. Everything to hand for camp or holing up, whatever the situation,' Tom grinned.

Ben clapped him on the back.

'Good man. I know I can trust you. Let's go for a last drink before we leave this godforsaken hole.'

Tom felt himself stiffen. Was that a warning from Ben or was it just his heightened imagination and his own conflicting emotions? He couldn't tell and he didn't really know what was happening to himself. He just knew he wasn't happy with the situation. Maybe he was outgrowing that desperate sense of still being involved in another kind of war, which meant riding roughshod over anyone who resisted and taking what they wanted as a right.

They were predators, without even the excuse of fighting for a cause.

He looked at Josh walking ahead with Ben and suddenly saw them both for what they were. Soulless zombies, both of them. Ben had the brains and could plan, and was as dangerous as a rattlesnake. He could easily kill his own brother if need be. As for Josh, he was just a big hulking piece of flesh with man's urges, no brains and no heart.

As for himself, what was he? He could kill.

He could think, and what he thought often disturbed his nights. He knew his mother would have been ashamed of him. His mind slithered over things he'd done of which he was ashamed. There was no doubt about it, the standards he'd been brought up with as a child were away above him. He, with the others, was on a devil's ride to hell.

He was quiet as they drank together in Griffin's bar. The barman was talkative and he was also curious.

'Where you headin' for gentlemen?'

'Goin' to try our luck with that cattle drive making for Abilene.'

The barman nodded as he leaned over and sopped up spilled beer from his bartop with a dirty grey dishcloth.

'Oh, you mean Sam Featherstone's outfit? I heard tell they wanted some extra hands. A mean outfit though. Doesn't believe in feedin' good vittles. Can't keep his men.'

Ben grunted.

'Good thing we've our own grub then. You know this Sam Featherstone?'

'Some. Been through several times. Doesn't pass through here, camps about ten miles away, but usually comes in for a poker session. Isn't a hard-drinkin' man. They say he's got a few families ridin' with him this time. Folks goin' to California. Somethin' new for him to take womenfolk along.'

'Womenfolk?'

The morose Josh brightened up and suddenly took an interest in the conversation, his moodiness forgotten.

'Yeh. The miserable old bastard must be makin' a fortune takin' on families.'

'How'd ya know all this?'

The barman laughed.

'The grapevine's faster than any telegraph, mister. We know what's goin' on all over the territory. We know when outlaws are moseying along, and when banks are moving their gold and when the President himself farts!'

'Do you now?' And Ben looked mighty thoughtful. 'You reckon those families carry more than just their possessions?'

The barman gave Ben a sly look. 'I reckon.'

'And what about Sam? Does he carry more than his bedroll?'

'Not if he was wise, he wouldn't. I reckon he gets his cash in Abilene when he unloads those cows. He'll need it then to pay off his men. So why the interest in other people's cash?'

Ben shrugged. 'I thought we might offer ourselves as guards rather than cowpokes.'

The barman gave a great belly laugh.

'I should like to see old Sam's face when you mention guards! He'll kick your arses to hell!'

But he didn't. Sam Featherstone rubbed his bristly cheek and looked Ben up and down when he made his proposal.

'Have you done this work before?'

'Yeh, we specialize in security work. Tom here is one of the fastest gunhawks I've ever seen and I've seen a helluva lot.'

'Hmm. Let's see what you can do, Tom.' Sam scooped up two wads of clay and threw them high into the sky, one after the other without further warning.

Tom crouched and drew, aimed and fired in one smooth movement. The clods of earth exploded showering back to earth. Sam Featherstone was impressed.

'Are you all as good as him?'

Ben smiled. 'We shouldn't be with him if we weren't,' he lied.

'So you do really specialize in security. No kid?'

'No kid.' Ben stared him straight in the eyes.

'Hmm, well I could use three good men. I might as well tell you now, we've been losin' beeves on the last three drives. That's why I've had to encumber myself with tender-foot families to recoup. I've had trouble with the men too. Seems like I pick 'em wrong. They argue and fight and some just up and leave during the night. What about you guys? Short-fused are you?'

Ben laughed and Tom gave a wry smile.

'Naw ... we lead a quiet life, don't we

Tom? Josh here is a bit hotheaded if he's crossed, but that's because he's young. We don't go lookin' for trouble.' He smiled again disarmingly.

'Right! You can all start right now. We're a bit thin on the flanks.'

'You mean we're riding drag?' Josh burst out. 'We're biting dust?' His face suffused with colour. Ben clapped a hard heavy hand about his shoulders and pressed warningly.

'Any reason why you shouldn't, mister?' Now Sam's voice was sharp.

Josh shrugged sullenly. 'Naw, I suppose not. You're the boss.' The pressure lifted off Josh's shoulders.

'Well, that's settled then. See you at tucker time.' Sam Featherstone rode off.

It only took a few days for Tom and Ben to realize that Sam Featherstone's outfit was divided within itself. There were those who had been with Sam for years and there were the newcomers, the itinerants, who were quietly disposed of if and when necessary.

Sam's segundo was a big quiet-moving

man called Ted Drydan. He looked to be a bar brawler and his beer gut showed where he got most of his entertainment. He was good at his job but Tom disliked him on sight. The man's round moon face bothered him. You never could tell what he was thinking. Tom put him down as a barrel of lard. But he was wrong. Ted was devious and hid it behind the moon mask he presented to the world at large.

It had been one of those long hard days in the saddle when storm clouds gathered and puffs of wind eddied and tried already raw nerves.

The cattle had been nervous too. The leaders chary of moving forward, the mavericks breaking cover and the cowboys ever on the alert to round up the strays and bring them back to the herd.

There had been much cursing and both men and horses were tired. Yet another night had to be gone through, and the herd not yet settled. They were needing water and probably could smell it in the wind.

Tom, who was doing the nightwatch with Ben moved slowly around the perimeter of the herd. He hummed a lullaby learned from his mother. Soon he would meet up with Ben and they could pause and talk and then move on. He looked at the stars which were partially obscured by clouds. Not a good night. It was a restless listening kind of night and not even a coyote called its mate.

He was thinking of the three families driving in the rear and at one side of the herd so that they escaped the perpetual cloud of dust engendered by 1,200 beeves.

Each man had his wife and they all had children along and all their possessions in sturdy conestoga wagons, which moved heavily and clumsily behind teams of horses.

One man's two teenage sons helped on the cattle drive. There were three young girls who helped the three wives cook the food for the outfit for that was part of the deal. The rest were young children, two small boys and a baby girl.

Josh had already got to know the girls and

it was this that was preoccupying Tom's mind: how to watch Josh and not upset him but keep the girls, Jessica, Sarah and Mary, safe. He would mention his fears to Ben when they met up and took their break.

He heard Ben's approach before he saw the moving figure on horseback.

'Hi, Ben,' he whispered, so as not to disturb the settling herd. 'How's tricks?'

Then the moon appeared for an instant as clouds dispersed and he saw that he was mistaken. This wasn't Ben. It was … and then a slight noise behind him made him turn in the saddle, but it was too late, the whole world crashed on his head and as he fell out of the saddle he had the impression that the cows nearest to him were heaving themselves on to their feet and he knew he was going to be trampled…

The pounding wasn't just in his head, it was all around him. He was lying a foot from a boulder which probably saved his life for the maddened cattle had obviously gone round it when they bolted.

He sat up and fingered the swelling at the back of his head. He felt the stickiness of blood. It had to be a killing blow to cause such damage for his stetson would have given partial protection.

Eyes, grown cold and grim and jaw set, he scrabbled around and found the remains of his hat. It had been pounded into the ground by countless hooves. It was now just a mess of black felt. He threw it away in disgust after he found the ten dollar gold eagle sewn in the lining.

He got to his feet. The dawn was coming up, yellow and pink streaks highlighting the fair mountains. The smell of cows was everywhere but not a cow to be seen.

Hell! What went wrong? Those cows had been more relaxed than they had been all day. Then he remembered the bulky figure which turned out not to be Ben. And what had become of Ben? Gradually it all came back. There wasn't only that bulky figure, there must have been others, at least the one who cold-cocked him. Anger rose in him.

Nobody crept up on Tom Hitchens and got away with it!

He walked and he cursed every step for his high-heeled riding boots weren't made for walking. He followed the trail and the sun was halfway high before he came up with the cook's wagon and a bunch of guys eating a much needed breakfast.

'And where the hell were you during the ruckus?' Sam Featherstone greeted him furiously. He looked drawn and tired and mighty furious. 'I thought you were the king-pin gunslinger. You know we were raided last night? Lost more than a hundred beeves!'

'I'm sorry. I got slammed from behind.' Sam's eyes were probing, assessing.

'If I thought you flunked out and was in on it, I'd...'

'You've only gotta feel the bump on my head...' began Tom furiously.

'That could be a deliberate act, feller. It's been known to happen so's a feller ain't suspected!'

'Aw, to hell with you! If you feel like that, me and my pards will ride out. It's no sweat on the rate of pay and your rotten grub! I'll pick up my gear and...'

'Hey, now, not so fast, feller. I said *could be* deliberate, not that it was. There's a difference, y'know.'

'Well, speak up. My head doesn't make for patience, Mr Featherstone, sir!'

'Right. We'll take it someone bounced you one, and you didn't see who?'

'Right. But if I find out who did it, then there's goin' to be trouble.'

'You think it was someone in the outfit?'

'Yeh, who else would know where I'd be at that time?' Suddenly something cold crept up and down Tom's spine and made the hair stand up on the back of his neck. There was only one man who knew where Tom would be ... Ben Kirby.

He stared hard at Sam Featherstone and not by a blink betrayed the fact that he might have answered his own question.

Sam Featherstone took off his hat and

scratched his head.

'How far can I trust you?'

Tom shrugged. 'Look, mister, you either trust me or you don't and at the moment I don't care which you do. All I know is that I was hired as a security guard and drover. I know bugger all about you and I couldn't care less. As long as you pay me, I'm your man. Right?'

'What about those pards of yours? The young 'un seems hotheaded crazy and his brother isn't far behind. I've heard their quarrelling with some of the men but I've stayed clear because I don't want to lose any more. We're still short-handed as it is.'

'You can count on them, Mr Featherstone. All we want is to get to Abilene, so's we can get on the next train bound for Texas.'

Sam Featherstone grunted.

'It ain't what it's cracked up to be in Texas. It's all wild cows and outlaws and the dregs from the cesspits. You'd be better off working for me, fulltime.'

Tom's laugh was harsh.

'What? At your rates? You think we're imbeciles? We're not out to make you rich, Mr Featherstone. We want a piece of the cake ourselves.'

'So it's no use talking to them?'

Tom shook his head. 'Our plans is made, mister. Our guns ... at least, my gun ... is yours until come Abilene.'

He thought of that conversation when he met up with Ben. There was something he had to know.

'Ben, we must talk.'

Ben looked at the grim face.

'Look, I had nothing to do with you being smashed over the head.'

'You knew it was going to happen?'

'Yeh, me and Ted Drydan got into a huddle. He was drunk and I helped him to get drunker and he had a proposition but I swear I didn't know that you were to be cold-cocked...'

'But it would look right if one of us caught it? I'd have you know, *pard*,' and he emphasized the word, 'that if it hadn't been for a dirty big boulder, those damn cows would have pounded me into mincemeat.'

'Look I'm sorry. You're in for a cut. Drydan's got it made. He's already taken out about five hundred head. That's why they're short-handed. Old Featherstone won't know until the tally in Abilene and then it'll be too late.'

'Is Josh in on this too?'

'Nope! That fool couldn't keep his mouth shut long enough. It's only you and me, Tom and Drydan and his crowd. We're on to a good thing, Tom. Think about it.'

'I've thought and I don't like it.'

'Hell, Tom, what's come over you? It's a snip!'

Tom turned away. He didn't want Ben to see the suspicion in his eyes.

'You want to throw in with Drydan then?'

'Yes. As I've said, we'll get us a bank-roll.' He laughed. 'Maybe we'll roll Drydan over and take the rest when we get to Abilene. What with Featherstone's stash and that of those families, we could be sitting pretty.'

Tom didn't stop to listen to the rest. Ben was making his gorge rise. He wondered why he'd followed him when they'd left Quantrill. He'd known what a bastard he was but in those days his own sensitivity had been blunted. Now, he was emerging as a different man.

SEVEN

Jessica Tully reminded Tom of Rosie Swindon. She had light-brown hair and blue eyes too. She was the oldest of the three sisters, and had a trim lithe figure. She worked efficiently with the older women and, when she served Tom along with the rest, her glance was frank and open.

'Thank you, Jessica,' he said as she handed him a tin plate of stew.

'You're welcome.' She moved on to Josh

who tried to hold her hand when she gave him his plate.

Tom saw the way she shrugged off the youth and he saw how the dull colour suffused his face. Josh didn't like Jessica's rebuff and neither did Ben for he too, much to Tom's surprise, was making clumsy overtures to the girl.

'She's an uppity bitch, that one,' Josh growled under his breath as he forked beef.

'You mind what you say, Josh. The gal's just bein' choosy. I've a mind for her myself.' Josh looked at Ben with surprise.

'You? I thought you liked 'em with experience, not young 'uns to be broke in.'

'Mmm,' he said, watching Jessica moving amongst the men and now dispensing coffee from a huge blackened metal urn which did duty as a coffee pot. 'Only because the old 'uns make less fuss. Some of 'em even welcome it!'

His white teeth gleamed amidst the black beard as he tore off a hunk of bread and began to chew, his eyes still on Jessica.

127

'You're really smitten with her,' marvelled Josh. 'Well, I'll be damned! We could share her. What you say?'

Ben frowned.

'Now to hell with that! Pick one of the others. They're both big enough so they're old enough.' He turned his head to the listening Tom. 'You can share with Tom, here.'

'You'd better think again, Ben. A rush of blood to the head like that, and all our plans will be down the Swannee.'

'Oh, I don't mean for us to take 'em right now, but we'll need some reward for playing nice guys for so long. We'll take 'em after we take that old bastard, Featherstone, for all he's got.'

'But we'll be nearly into Abilene by then!' Tom protested.

Ben gave him a slanting glance. 'Don't you like the idea, Tom? Or are you impatient to get at the girls that much sooner?'

Tom spat on the ground, his stomach muscles knotted.

'You know like hell what I mean. You don't go about raping women right near Abilene.'

'No, we do it when they leave Abilene. They'll probably want to hire us to take them to California.'

'Hell, Ben, we're not going to California.'

'I know, we all know, but they don't! Simple. And don't forget, each family has a strong-box stashed away, or are you so dumb you've forgotten that interesting fact?'

Tom didn't answer but scraped what was left on his plate to the ground and, heaving himself upright, took the plate to a pile of dirty dishes and without a look at Jessica or the other women, moved away to drink another mug of coffee and ponder on Ben's plan.

He was a cold, cruel bastard and something was going to have to be done. He stared hard into the setting sun, not seeing it. He cursed Ben and he cursed the day he'd been sweet-talked into following him with that spiel about surviving and being smart after the war and taking what you want as a right. He'd been a mad-dog fool at that time, brainwashed as a Confederate fighting machine without conscience or humanity in him. Now, his conscience was working overtime.

He stirred and blinked as a figure stood before him. It was Jessica.

'Hello. Mrs Jennings sent me over to ask if you weren't feeling well. She saw you tip most of your stew away. She's got a remedy for an upset stomach.' She smiled apologetically. 'I'm sorry to disturb you. Maybe you just want to be alone.'

'No. You're not disturbing me, and I'm not ill.'

'Mrs Jennings is in charge of the cooking and she gets upset about the poor quality dry goods we've got to work with. Says if she'd known what a mean skunk Mr Featherstone was, she'd have advised Mr Jennings not to accompany him but wait for the next wagon-train.'

Tom smiled up at her. 'Well, you can tell

Mrs Jennings that I've eaten worse grub than what she provides. I suppose you eat different to us?'

'Oh, yes. We all have our own provisions. We only cook for the outfit. I'm sorry it's so dull and there's weevils in the flour...'

'Not your fault, miss. Forget it.'

There was a pause and she looked down at her feet and she scuffed one foot, drawing a pattern in the dirt.

'I didn't come over just to give you Mrs Jennings' message.'

'Oh? What did you really come for?'

'It's those men you ride with. They frighten me. They're always watching me and it makes me...' She stopped and shuddered.

Tom's heart sank. He'd hoped she'd be too naïve to even take notice of the lecherous looks, the sly innuendoes, apart from the touching of hands.

'I'm sorry,' he said evenly, 'it's just the way they are. They mean no harm.' God forgive him for that lie. 'But I'll warn them. I'll watch out for you, miss.'

She rewarded him with a brilliant smile.

'Oh would you? I was sure I could trust you. You're so different from them.' She bit her lip and then blurted out. 'They frighten my sisters too and Sara is only thirteen and Mary is twelve. They shouldn't even know what to be frightened of at their age!'

'As I said, I'm sorry, miss, and I'll do what I can. Just make sure you never walk alone out in the bush … you know, for what you have to do. Take someone with you. Right?'

Jessica blushed. 'Oh! Thank you very much!' She turned and ran back to the fire. Tom smiled. The tactful reference to bodily functions had sure upset her. Then he frowned. What the hell would it be like for her if she was ever subjected to what Ben or Josh could do to her?

At least he had time to think out a plan of action before they reached Abilene. It would mean taking those teenage youths into his confidence and maybe spiriting the girls away before they ever came anywhere near

Abilene. He would have to think it out carefully.

He considered putting Featherstone in the picture but that old bastard wasn't worth helping and he wasn't too sure who was with Ted Drydan and his gang and who was a hundred per cent loyal to the old man. It could mean total warfare and a herd stampeding and everyone ending up with nothing. No, it meant some careful planning.

But he was wrong.

They were on their fourth week of cattle-driving and Tom was pairing off with one of the teenage sons of Chas Williams, the leader of the families going to California. They were nighthawks and quietly doing their rounds and Tom was humming his usual lullaby.

All was still. The partial moon had just come up and there was a clear blue-black night sky. Visibility was good although the shadows were intense. Tom's arse was sore. He was suffering with piles, a hazard for all cowboys who lived in the saddle. The itch kept him from nodding as his mount moved automatically around the sleeping herd.

Suddenly he heard a faint scream and his head snapped up. What the hell? Then distinctly he heard the sound of horses galloping and the sound grew fainter as they moved rapidly away.

He heard a horse trotting towards him, and a voice called out, 'Are you there, Tom?' He recognized the boyish tones of Bob Williams, as he crashed through the brush.

'Yeh, I'm here all right.'

'Did you hear that screamin'? I think it came from one of the wagons. What should we do, Tom? Should we leave the herd and go and find out?'

'Look, boy, we don't want to get the herd steamed up. You crashin' through the under-growth as you did was enough to set 'em off. It's a damn good thing it's not a spooky night with wind! Now you just set yourself here and carry on singin' to the ornery bastards and I'll take a looksee. Right?'

'OK if you say so, Tom. Chico and Luke are due to take over at two, so I'll see you then.'

'If it's anythin' serious, Bob, you pa will be in on it, and Mr Tully and George Hanks.'

Bob nodded, half sorry he wasn't the one to go and investigate, and half glad he wasn't for fear it was raiders after the cattle, but as the herd seemed peaceful, he was sure it was nothing to do with rustling.

He watched Tom trot away quietly so as not to spook the herd. There were a few raised heads and a bit of bawling and one maverick steer actually got to his feet and bellowed to the moon. Bob held his breath. He'd never been alone with a herd that might spook. But the maverick settled and all was still.

Tom found pandemonium amongst the three conestoga wagons that were drawn up well away from the herd and the herd's outfit. Everyone was up, even the baby was awake in the Hanks' wagon.

The womenfolk were huddled round a

dying fire comforting one of their number, while George Hanks and Chas Williams tended a bloodied Aaron Tully.

'What happened?' Tom gazed down at the three men.

'Two masked raiders broke into our wagon,' gasped Aaron Tully, 'and dragged Jessica and Sarah out of bed and just rode off with them! God damn them to hell! They didn't even want money when I offered it to them to leave them alone. All I got was a slash over the head for my pains and when Minnie tried to interfere they hit her too. I don't understand it! How the hell would outsiders know about Jessica and Sarah, for God's sake?'

Tom's blood ran cold. He knew who would know.

'Anyone out there followin' them?'

'There's only us. The other camp's too far away and it's been so sudden we haven't got organized.' Williams and Hanks looked helplessly at each other and at the distraught father.

'Right! I'm going after them.'

'But how can you? You'll never keep up with their trail in the dark!'

'I'll manage. I've got an inbuilt instinct for trailing. Something to do with my old grandmother!'

He raked his horse's mouth to turn him in the direction he figured to travel. A woman muffled in a huge shawl broke free from the other women and staggered towards him.

He saw she was bleeding down the side of her face. She was in a bad way but she was determined. He recognized her as Jessica's mother.

'Mr Hitchens!'

'Yes, Mrs Tully?'

'You're going after my girls, aren't you? Jessica told me all about you and that she could trust you. Do you think it's those friends of yours who've taken them away?' She swayed as she spoke.

'I don't know, ma'am, but whoever they are, I'll find them and kill them, ma'am, and I'll bring your girls back. That I'll promise.'

'Bless you, Mr Hitchens.'

'Now you go and let those ladies look after you and don't fret none. I'll find 'em,' he said, and dug his heels into the horse's ribs and the great beast leapt forward.

He wasn't so confident as he'd made out. Oh, he'd find them all right, but he could hardly point out to Mrs Tully that he might find them too late. Jessica and Sarah could be ravished because he knew what drink did to the Kirby brothers and Ben must have indulged in one of his rare binges to endanger his long-term plan.

Tom cursed him to hell. Ben cockproud meant Josh would be the same. There would be no way of stopping Josh when Ben was in that foolhardy randy mood. It was as if the floodgates opened and all Ben's iron control was washed away leaving him like a frustrated stallion. Even his brains and cunning left him when he was in this state.

Trying to thwart him would be like facing a cougar.

Tom rode fast in the direction he

remembered of the galloping hooves. Then he cut trail and spent time crossing and recrossing the terrain and the moon sailed higher and it became easier.

At last he found the imprints of two sets of hooves. He was on the right track. He wondered just how far they would travel before lust overcame them. Any old where would do when they were in that frenzied state. He remembered incidents during the war ... but he didn't want to remember all those gory details. What he had to remember was that they were two animals with a ruthless sex drive and if they got started, he didn't fancy those poor girls' chances.

The first streaks of sunrise were showing when finally he caught up with them. At first he heard a long low muling sound which chilled his blood. It was the cry of a kitten in pain.

He hauled on the reins and listened, his eyes not leaving the telltale ground. It had taken him quite a time to keep to the trail, losing it over rock and wasting time tracking crisscross until he hit the telltale signs again.

Now he listened, jaw grim and the smothered shriek had him dismounting fast. He tethered his horse well away from the sound and looked to his Colt feeding it slugs. Then, he crept forward and now his natural ability came to his aid. Down on his belly, he slithered forward, easing himself without disturbing a mouse or a stone. He had the patience of the Blackfoot and he got to within twenty yards of the two men who were between him and a small nearly extinct fire. They were two black figures etched against the dim glow of wood embers.

One crouched low as the other watched. Tom saw and heard the slap of a hand against a cheek.

'Aw, give it up, Ben. She's no good now. We've worn her out.' Tom watched as the standing figure tipped a bottle and drank and then he looked at the bottle and threw it away. 'We're out of liquor, Benny boy. Hey, Ben...'

But Ben was scooping up the inert figure

of a girl and peering closely into her face. Then he dropped her at his feet and passed a shaking hand across his forehead.

'Hell! This one's snuffed it too. Bloody well cheated on us, and us not halfway done! It's your fault, Josh, you were too rough.'

'Me? Why, you bastard, you couldn't get at it quick enough! When it comes to some real screwing, you're a bloody stallion. I know what's with you, Benny boy, you've got to have them screamin' before you get at it, but when you do...'

'Shurrup, and let me think. We can't go back as if we've been out huntin' the girls. That bastard, Tom wouldn't believe it for one. Too risky.'

'Aw, stop worryin'. We've always made out. You always come up with somethin'.'

'Not this time he don't!' Tom said and rose up from the cover of a group of small boulders. His gun blasted but Ben and Josh reacted simultaneously and ducked and dived, scrabbling for their guns.

Ben's gun spat as Josh tugged and pulled at his weapon, Ben narrowly missing Tom's ear. Tom rolled and came up shooting and Josh yelped and Tom heard him curse.

Then his attention was on Ben, this furious fighting Ben who had always fought his battles during the war like a ferocious animal. Coolly Tom waited for Ben's attack. It would come like it always did without warning, deadly with the precision of a general's planning.

It came from his left side. Ben was a past master at Indian fighting. Tom removed himself to a new position, his quick ear listening for the betraying sounds. Suddenly Ben was nearly on top of him, his gun firing twice and on the third click, Tom knew it was empty. Then, as Ben tossed away the gun they were grappling together rolling over and over until they came to the crumpled body of the girl and then Tom felt a surge of power in him.

'You bastard!' he growled as he gouged at Ben's eyes and then caught a glancing blow to the groin which sent the breath gusting from him. Then he was landing blows to the side of Ben's head. 'You gonna pay for this. A bullet's too quick for such as you!' he panted.

'Is that why you didn't just shoot us down?' The mocking tone set Tom's teeth on edge, and he clawed for Ben's throat.

'You got it in one, Ben Kirby,' and he slammed Ben's head hard against the ground and then found himself catapulted on to his back as Ben Kirby heaved and kicked upwards, and before he could draw air into his lungs, Ben was on him like a tearing, rending cougar.

Pain sliced through him as Ben's knuckles caught his nose, smashing it causing blood to fill his mouth to choke him. He spat and ducked and caught Ben in the solar plexus. For a moment both men lay gasping air and then Ben's outstretched fingers closed round a huge rock and he was in the act of heaving it at Tom when Tom went for his gun.

The shot took Ben in the forehead. The rock slammed down and caught Tom on the left shoulder, numbing it.

It was then that Josh, shoulder bleeding, dragged himself towards Tom, his gun held waveringly in his hand as he tried to aim at Tom, but it was too much for him and he collapsed near Ben.

Tom staggered to his feet like a drunken man. His legs were like jelly and he was sure he had a broken rib.

He looked at Ben.

'So long ol' pard. I always knew it would come to this,' he said, and he tottered to where Josh was lying. 'You too, Josh. You were born to be killed.'

He forced his jelly legs to move away from the two bodies before he collapsed. The sun was high when he came to, and he could hear the buzz of flies and it all came back. The two Kirby brothers were dead.

There were flies buzzing about the blood on his face. It was black and congealed and his mouth tasted like a cow's arse. He lay awhile until the world stopped spinning and then he tried to rise and his busted rib gave him hell. But once upright, he felt a little better after he threw up a mess of blood which looked like liver.

He would have given all his pay for a panniken of water to drink and sluice his head with. But the terrain was dry. There was no convenient little stream to ease his condition. He gritted his teeth in the effort it took to move. He must find those girls and take them back to their families...

Sarah was easy to find. She lay beside the now dead fire, her body partly naked and bruised and her face showing marks of ill-usage. She must have fought hard before she was subdued and raped.

Tom was conscious of great rage. He'd let those girls down. He hadn't been able to save them despite his promises to Jessica. Something inside him wanted to explode. He could well understand the Indians who took revenge on an enemy's body even after death.

It took some time before he was capable of looking for Jessica.

He found her half buried under brush-wood. The innocence and gaiety long gone. She looked like an old woman. Her hands were torn and bleeding and there were the marks of rope burns on her wrists. The dogs had tied her down, and they, like animals had bitten her all over.

He was ill again before he could lift her up tenderly and carry her to where her sister lay. Then he found the tethered horses and stowed each body as circumspectly as he could in the circumstances.

The horses balked at the unusual burdens but finally he managed to reach his own horse and tethering each horse to the tail of the one in front started the sad little cavalcade back to the grieving families.

They moved at walking pace. He was in no hurry to bring unhappiness to these good people. He dreaded it, but it had to be done.

Grimly he moved on and while he did so, he reviewed his whole life. He was sick at heart. If only he had taken things into his own hands when he first found that he and the Kirbys had nothing in common! Then these girls would still be alive. He judged himself a coward, a man who didn't want to face up to what he'd become.

A coward, he kept telling himself. A no-good sonofabitch who didn't deserve to live!

When he finally came in sight of the three conestoga wagons and all the adults came running to meet him, he knew what he was to do. He would go back to Kentucky and look for Rosie and it would be up to her if he was to settle down. The choice would be hers.

Aaron Tully was running ahead of the rest, then he slowed down and Tom saw his shoulders sag. Then the man was rooted to the spot, staring with tears rolling down his face.

'You … you found them?' His voice was a whisper.

A hard lump filled Tom's throat. He could only nod and move on, with Aaron Tully holding on to the bridle of his oldest daughter.

The small crowd surrounded them but kept a respectful distance. Then came the dreadful keening of the women and the girls' mother fainted. Jessica and Sarah were home.

EIGHT

The world suddenly rocked and went black and when Tom opened his eyes, it was to see a ring of faces looking down at him.

'What happened?' He passed a swollen tongue across cracked and broken lips and someone raised his head and sloshed water into his mouth, while someone in the background said, 'Gently does it, fellers, too much will bust his guts.'

He licked his lips, too tired to care what was happening to him and closed his eyes because looking upwards was making his stomach heave.

They were moving him when he passed out from the pain in his rib and his shoulder and when he came to again he was in one of the wagons and a strange woman was tending him.

She smiled at him, a pleasant plump woman in her forties.

'I'm Mrs Jennings and I'm glad to see you awake. I thought we were going to lose you. Would you like some soup?'

Tom licked his lips, no longer dry and he wasn't thirsty, but at the mention of soup, his guts responded.

'Yes, I could take some soup.'

But when he tried to hold the mug and drink for himself, he found he was too weak. Mrs Jennings carefully held the mug so that he could drink.

The effort was nearly too much and Tom's head flopped back on the striped black and white tick pillow.

'There now, you've done very well,

considering.' Mrs Jennings beamed and turned to move away. Tom caught her skirt, and she turned back to him. 'What is it?'

'The girls...?'

Mrs Jennings' pleasant face clouded over.

'Mr and Mrs Tully buried them yesterday. They wanted it that way.'

'And the Kirby brothers?'

'My husband and some of the men rode out but couldn't find the location. I'm afraid they'll not get a proper burial, Tom.'

Tom nodded. They would be crowbait by now and what was left would be for the maggots.

'I'll have to get up and get movin', Mrs Jennings, ma'am. I'm leavin' as soon as possible.'

'You can't possibly leave yet! Your rib will take a while and your shoulder muscles were torn and as for your face...'

Tom detected a note of ... was it pity? ... in her voice.

'What about my face?' It felt swollen and he knew he'd had trouble breathing during the last few days.

'Well, you broke your nose…'

'Yeh, I remember that, but what's a broken nose? It's nothin' to worry about. Is it?'

'Well, it's not a pretty sight and you're going to have a scar and it's not healing well.'

'Have you a mirror?'

Mrs Jennings nodded. 'Yes, but…'

'Let me have it … please.'

Reluctantly Mrs Jennings produced a small mirror and Tom surveyed his battered features for a long moment. He'd been roughly shaved so that his face wound could be tended and thus the misshapen nose and the swollen puckered cheek could not be hidden.

Tom was conscious of repulsion. It was like looking at some hideous mask. This wasn't Tom Hitchens, this was someone come back from hell!

He flung the mirror to the bottom of the bed.

'I've got to go.' He struggled upright and flung back the bedclothes despite being naked underneath and in the presence of a woman. After all, Mrs Jennings must know every inch of his body if she'd been his nurse since he collapsed.

'Tom, for God's sake, you're in no fit state to look after yourself. That wound on your face needs attention.'

'I'll live! I just don't want to see the same kind of pity on everyone's face as I see in yours!'

'Then wait just a few more days!'

'No. I'm going now. Where's my clothes?'

Silently she pointed to a pile of cleaned and mended clothes and he reached for his long johns. He was dizzy, but he hid his weakness and Mrs Jennings left him, only to return some time later with her husband.

'Tom, I understand you want to leave. Are you sure that's a good idea at the moment?'

'I'm sorry. I've got to go. It's not only my face. I'm sure I'd frighten all the kids, it's something else. They were my pards, and I was riding with them when they took those girls. I can't face their folks. I've got to go.'

Mr Jennings put a hand on Tom's shoulder.

'I understand. But I want you to know that none of us blames you along with them bastards. Mr Featherstone says your job with us is waitin' for you when you're ready.'

Tom shook his head, his gaze on his feet.

'It wouldn't work. But thank him for me, and thanks to you, Mrs Jennings, ma'am, for what you done for me.'

Mrs Jennings nodded and bit her lip.

'Are you sure about this? You're in no fit state.'

'I'm sure, ma'am, thank you kindly.'

'Then I'll pack you some food.' She left the wagon.

'Tom I understand how you feel, but...'

'Look, Mr Jennings, there's no way I can go on to Abilene. I've got something to put right back east. I'm goin' back.'

Mr Jennings gave him a long hard look. Then, 'You sure have made your mind up. I'll see your horse is saddled and the missis will find you a blanket and a frypan and the usual utensils. You'll want a coffee pot.'

'That's thoughtful of you. I can pay.'

'Forget it! What you did was somethin' I couldn't ... wouldn't have tackled even if it had been my own wife! I'm no man of action and you knew what you were getting yourself into. No, boy, I reckon the Tullys will see it as we do.'

'I can't face them, Mrs Jennings. The men who killed their girls were men I rode with and I should have known that sooner or later they would go for those girls. I should have seen it comin'.'

'You can't blame yourself, son. It was the Lord's will.'

'The Lord's will, hell!' Tom spoke savagely. 'Those girls would be alive now if I'd done something about it! I didn't reckon on Ben getting drunk with Josh when I was doin' nighthawk! I should have warned you all what they were capable of! God! How I hate myself!'

Mr Jennings looked with pity at Tom's bowed head.

'Son, we all have things we're sorry for. I think it would be better if you did go out into them there hills and purge all the bitterness out of yuh, then start again. You're doin' right to go. But we'll miss yuh,' he said, and with that he left the wagon.

Tom thought long about the Jennings and the Tullys and the rest as he rode east. They were the salt of the earth; good, honest, kind people and it was hard coming to terms with what happened.

He rode with the sun at his back as he slowly backtrailed. He avoided the small settlements. He wasn't ready for man's company. Neither was he used to riding alone but he found it strangely exhilarating to pit his wits against whatever might come up. It was a matter of survival. He took his time. He found that old instincts surfaced. The blood of his Indian grandmother predominated and he realized an affinity with the rugged wild country, that he'd never suspected.

Sometimes he found himself looking back

as he rode. There was a spot in the middle of his back that itched now and again. It was as if he was being watched.

Mrs Jennings' package of food lasted several days but now he was reduced to using the flour and salt she'd provided along with a sack of beans. He tried out the old rifle Mr Jennings had slipped into the boot below the saddle. There was a box of cartridges in amongst his dry goods too. He blessed the good man's thoughtfulness and though the gun wasn't as good as the army rifle he'd lost, it was accurate, for he brought down several jack-rabbits and a half-grown buck which supplemented his food supply.

He was satisfied that he could travel for weeks before hitting a town for further supplies.

It was a healing time. He put the whole sorry episode into some kind of perspective. He still blamed himself for not dealing with Ben Kirby and his brother earlier. He'd always expected a showdown at some time, but he never envisaged the two brothers uniting in the act of kidnapping the two young sisters from a family they were travelling with. Ben had always been concerned about Josh. He was the one with the problem.

No matter how Tom brooded on it, he could never figure it. It must have been the drink that unleashed all Ben's frustrated passions. That and Josh's taunts about Ben's lack of libido. That was the only conclusion Tom could come up with.

Tom crouched over the small fire, mulling over the same sickening events until he was nearly crazy. He was roasting a rabbit spitted on a stick. He stared at the blackened meat as he turned it. It was nearly done and the smell of it plus the boiling coffee rumbled his guts.

His mare was tethered close by, head down and pulling a clump of dried grass. Suddenly her head came up, ears twitching and she gave a low nicker as of welcome. There was no hint of alarm.

Tom, the rabbit dropping to the ground,

rose to his feet and his hand went for his Colt, the rifle leaning against a rock but too far away to be useful.

He catfooted to where the horse was standing and saw she was staring into the brush.

'What is it, old girl?'

She rubbed her nose against his hand, and then pricked up her ears again. Tom waited, his ears aching with the effort of listening. But there was only the sound of the light breeze.

He patted the mare.

'Missing your running mates? Is that it?' he said, then went back to the fire and retrieved his rabbit and ate, his senses alert. He drank coffee and then, for safety's sake, he scattered the remains of the fire and covered the ash with soil. A night fire made a man a good target. He wanted no nocturnal visitor, if there was one, to come upon him as he slept.

To satisfy himself, he took a last look around. He moved in ever widening circles around his camp but couldn't see any telltale signs of an intruder but he couldn't be sure because of the fitful moonlight.

Maybe the mare was just acting spooked. She too wasn't used to riding alone. She could be missing Ben and Josh's horses.

At last he turned in, satisfied that he was alone and no crazy drifter was trailing him. Yet he'd had those itchy feelings in his back and that fact kept him awake until nearly dawn.

The sun was well up when he made a move. He ate the rest of the rabbit and did without coffee but drank from his canteen before watering the mare. Then he was on his way.

He watched his back, but there were no telltale signs of rising dustclouds or any movement of any kind, not even a hawk sweeping the sky for prey. He was alone in a rugged wilderness.

He moved on slowly, giving the mare time to eat and rest for she'd been worked hard and she always gave of her best. He was beginning to heal and now the only problem was the suppurating wound on his cheek and he reckoned it was because his beard was growing about it and there must be poison in it. His nose was less swollen but because of the breakage, his nasal passage was obstructed. He would probably always have trouble with it. Other guys with broken noses had complained about that.

He came to a small stream and around it was a stand of pines and scrub, like an oasis with rich green grass growing on both banks. The green was restful to the eyes after days of peering into hot sunlight at a harsh sun-dried landscape. Tom decided to make camp and rest up for a few days.

He would do a bit of hunting. The game would be attracted to the water. It should be easy. He also wanted to attend to his face and scrape off his beard and give that wound a real chance to heal. He was becoming worried about it. It pained him and it smelled bad.

But first there were other chores. He took

a looksee and found to his relief that it didn't look as if he'd stumbled on a well-known watering place. He groomed the mare and cleaned her feet and noted the worn shoes and knew he would have to find a blacksmith to renew them soon.

Then he cleaned and oiled his guns before going after game. It was surprisingly hard to come by. Twice he saw deer in the distance but he could not get near enough to take a shot.

Several days went by and he'd only bagged a couple of rabbits. Then came the luck. He shot a tough old stag who'd caught his antlers in the thick undergrowth. He dragged it back to camp to skin and cut up.

It was a long messy job but when he straightened his aching back, he was well satisfied with the mound of joints and strips of meat ready for drying in the sun.

He made a bigger fire than usual and fashioned a tripod and hung up several choice joints to roast. Then he decided on the long promised bath in the clean mountain stream. He would wash his clothes too, for they were both travel-stained and bloody.

The water was icy cold but invigorating and he had the strange feeling he was sloughing off the past as the stink left him. He wished he had Mrs Jennings' mirror when he tackled his beard and the part around the wound gave him hell, but he was satisfied that the rough job he'd made of it wasn't too bad. It was pleasant to have the sun on his back and he was humming quietly to himself when a woman's voice said quietly, 'Don't make no move, white man, or I'll blow you to hell!'

Tom froze. He was in the act of bending down to pick up his long johns. He cursed silently for his rifle was leaning against a boulder and too far away to get at. Whoever she was, she'd crept up as silently as a cat and nicked his handgun while he'd been absorbed in cleaning up his face.

'Who are you and what do you want?' he bellowed sharply.

For a moment he thought she wasn't going to answer. Then, 'I want food. I smelled your meat roasting.'

Tom relaxed and started to turn and then remembered he was as naked as the day he was born, and stood still.

'You can have food and there's no need to point my own gun at me.'

'I'm sorry. I don't trust white men.'

'Then what are you going to do? Kill me before you eat?'

'I don't know. You look like a bad man.'

'Oh, hell! You can't go on looks. I've told you, take what you want and leave, but don't take my gun. I need it.'

'I've got a child back there in the scrub. She needs food as I do. I want to trust you...'

'Then either trust me or kill me for I'm damned if I'm goin' to stand here all day showin' you my arse. Can I move to pick up my underpants? I feel at a disadvantage like this.'

There was silence. He waited, and then at

a muffled gasp, he risked a sideways glance and was just in time to see a body slump to the ground and the metallic sound of his gun bouncing on the earth.

He leapt for his still damp pants and watching the inert body for signs of life, he dressed quickly, shrugging vest and shirt on with numbed fingers. That stream was decidedly cold.

He knelt beside her. She wasn't a young woman. Her black hair was streaked with grey but she was still comely. Her robe was of soft well-tanned leather embellished with symbols and porcupine quills, now sadly worn. She was dirty and unkempt and her moccasins showed age. He saw the signs of malnutrition.

Her eyes flickered open as he gathered her up to carry her to his camp.

'What you do with me?' Her voice was faint and fearful.

'I'm goin' to get you some food. What else?'

He felt her body shiver.

'You are white man. You take body.'

He let her down sharply on to his own blanket. He did not answer her but went and got his canteen.

'You drink a little, while I rustle you some grub. There's coffee when you're ready.'

She looked at him wide-eyed.

'You not want me?'

'Nope! Are you insulted?'

'Of course not. I thought all white men...' and she started to cry, and then she was struggling to her feet. 'I must fetch Aieda.'

'Sit yourself still and I'll go fetch her if you tell me where she is.'

'No! She will be frightened after what the strange white man did, and you ... you carry the devil's mark on your face!'

There was a courage about her as she spoke, as if waiting for a violent reaction from him. He laughed bitterly.

'Yeh, you might say the devil put his mark on me. But what of this man you speak of? Who was he?'

'He came three nights ago for food. My

son brought his wife away from our village to bear her new baby alone. I came to assist her and Aieda came with us. I had taken Aieda to look for the lichen needed to clot the blood. My son was paying homage to the Great Spirit for the safe arrival of the child. I could hear his chanting from far away. Suddenly it stopped.'

Slow tears welled in the woman's eyes.

'Then what happened?'

'I thought Lulalla was giving birth and so I rushed back. But I knew something was wrong when I saw my son moving backwards from the white man. He was holding a gun in one hand and what was left of a joint of meat with the other. He kept tearing at it with his teeth and he was laughing. I think he was whisky drunk like those men who hang around saloons.'

'And then?'

'Lulalla gave a great cry and my son leapt at the man who shot him and when he was down on the ground, the man shot him one, two, three more times and my son jerked and danced and the man laughed like crazy until my son was still.'

'What about your daughter-in-law?'

'I was going to run to her but I stayed hidden with Aieda for he went straight to the tepee and I heard the one shot. Then the man came out and took all the food and anything he could carry away on his horse and our three. Then he fired the tepee and rode away.'

'And you've been wandering ever since?'

She nodded and her head dropped to her chin.

Tom put a hand on her shoulder. He could feel her shudder.

'You go and bring the child and have no fear. I will prepare some food.'

He made panbread and warmed up last night's remains of the meat, his mind busy about what she'd told him. So there was a lone wolf skulking around who might be dangerous to himself. A crazy man, a survivor who'd turned into a predator. He'd have to go hunt him before he could leave these two alone in this unforgiving land.

He watched the small dark-eyed girl cling to her grandmother as she was brought to the fire. Her first glance at him showed her fear and it wasn't just because he was white. It was because of his face. One more reason why he should hide away somewhere and shun strangers.

He turned away as they ate ravenously and brewed more coffee.

Later he broached his plan to go hunt the killer but the woman smiled and drew herself up proudly.

'The Kiowa-Apache look after their own.'

'How will you do that?'

'You are a good man. Will you take us to our village? We have already walked far.'

'How much farther?'

'One ... two days. Then our braves will hunt this man down and we shall punish him well before he dies!'

Tom shuddered. He'd heard about the nasty habits of Indian squaws when they were out for vengeance.

'I'll take you,' he said abruptly and poured more coffee for them both. He nodded at the small girl now sound asleep. 'You will be her mother?'

'Of course. She is part of me.'

'Good. Then we'll start off at dawn.'

'But first there is something I must do.' The woman drew out a medicine bag that was hanging on a leather thong about her neck. Tom watched curiously as she drew the strings open and drew out several small bundles.

Then without a word, she turned away and busied herself mixing several herbs together. She rinsed out the coffee-pot and boiled a small amount of water and then added what smelled like buffalo fat to the noisome mixture and stirred it well. Then she poured the lot into Tom's tin mug and turned to him.

'When it is cooled and set I shall smear some on to your nose and cheek. It will draw out the poison. Now go and wash well and scrape off your beard.'

Tom did as he was told and within the hour he was lying by the fire, head on his saddle and she was plastering a thick greeny-yellow gunge all over his face. It stung and it smelled bad but he endured it for this woman seemed to know what she was about.

In the morning he found that it had set like wax and he had a hard job peeling off the caked mess. It brought with it all the scabby caked blood and the dried on pus. It hurt like hell and it bled but now it was clean red blood. The woman nodded, well satisfied.

'You will leave the surface free for the air to dry it. Tonight and every night you will plaster your face as I have done so, until all is used and then your face will heal naturally.'

'You really think so?'

'Already the angry flesh responds. The poison is stopped from spreading. You will see, it will be healed in several days.'

'What about my nose?'

'I'm sorry. The smashed bones have set. You will always carry scars but' – and now she smiled – 'you will not frighten little children any more!'

'Thank you for that. I thought a canker was eating my flesh away.'

'It was. Within weeks you would have been dead.'

Tom thought of these things as he walked beside his horse which carried the woman and the child and his camping equipment wrapped up in his blanket.

He trod warily, his eyes watching for any movement. None came and gradually he relaxed. It took the rest of the day and part of the next before they came in sight of the Indian village which consisted of several tepees grouped together.

He brought the horse to a standstill and looked at the woman gravely.

'This is where we part. Thank you for what you did for me. The throbbing in my face is easier. I shall do as you say.'

She smiled. 'And thank you for your help.

May you find what you look for.'

He started. 'What do you mean?'

'You know. It is there in your heart for anyone to see. Your destiny is far from here. Will you stay and eat with us?'

Tom shook his head. Several stalwart braves were waiting and though he would have their approval because of the squaw, he was in no mind to take up her offer.

'Thank you, but I shall ride on. I have far to go.'

'Very well. The spirits of the trees and water go with you as will those of the land itself.'

He turned and rode on and then at the bend in the trail, he looked back and she and Aieda waved and then moved purposefully towards the village.

He smiled to himself as he rode. The waving of hands in friendship felt good. It lightened the terrible burden of guilt he carried because of the Tully girls. Perhaps he was on the road back from hell...

NINE

Instinct was bringing him back to familiar country. It had been a time of inner contemplation, of getting back to nature. Except for stopping to have the mare reshod in a small hamlet with a crudely painted sign that proclaimed he was now in the township of Gerrard's Crossing, he had shunned his fellow men.

He'd stocked up on necessaries and tucked a bottle of whiskey into his saddle-bags as a luxury. He wasn't a hard drinker. Now as he studied the landscape before him, he knew that soon he would be back in that strange lonely valley.

His thoughts went before him. Would she still be there? And was she as pretty as he remembered her? Then, remembering his resolve just to make certain she wasn't living alone and that he would be leaving pronto, he firmly put all dangerous thoughts aside. He was no way another Josh Kirby who'd lived as a beast and reckoned women were only good for one thing.

Josh Kirby...

He should have checked on that bastard.

He'd only presumed he was dead because he'd shot him and seen him go down.

But the aftermath of all that had been hazy. He could hardly remember bringing those girls home for the Tullys to bury.

But he should have made sure.

He shrugged the thoughts aside as he studied the panoramic view before him. Now this was the country to settle in. He now knew that the day he threw in with Quantrill's ex-guerillas was the day he left Kansas for good.

He could never go back. His destiny was elsewhere, but where?

But first, he must see Rosie once more and put his mind to rest. He recognized the drift of the land. He was already riding towards the foothills that led to the secret mountain retreat and the lonely cabin on the edge of nowhere.

Unconsciously he kicked his heels into a gallop and the grand old mare responded and lengthened her stride and they travelled onwards towards an ever widening valley. Then the ground rose sharply as it rolled away into the coarse green pasture and Tom knew he wasn't very far away.

But now night was falling and it wouldn't do to approach the cabin in the dark. A chance shot without warning and he could be dead or crippled before questions were asked.

He made camp and now being confident, was careless of showing his fire. He was nearly home and dry. He could relax, take a drink and sleep without keeping one ear cocked.

It was a mistake. He woke with the distinct impression that someone was moving near him. There was a man stench close by. He rolled over and grabbed for his Colt. He listened but all was still.

Cursing himself for a fool he rose to his knees, Colt cocked.

'Is there anyone there?' he said, and, as a warning, let off a couple of warning shots.

No answer but the sighing of the breeze and a twittering of disturbed birds. Had he really heard someone, or was he going a bit loco?

Dawn broke and he got his answer. His depleted sack of coffee was gone as was the remains of his flour and beans and salt.

He didn't even have a chew of panbread or a mouthful of water.

He stared down at the empty saddle-bags. So he'd been right all along. His itchy back hadn't been wrong. There was a stalker back there and now the bastard was short on grub. But why stalk him like a cougar, keeping his distance and not challenging him? It didn't make sense.

He had the uneasy feeling that he could have been shot many times over. What was the object if whoever it was didn't want to kill him?

Tom broke camp thoughtfully. One thing was for sure. Whoever was stalking him didn't shy from the act of killing. He must have been the stranger who killed the Indians.

Anger boiled up in him. Whoever it was playing games with him would now have to watch out. It was one thing stalking someone who didn't know it, but a different setup when the victim was aware and ready to fight back!

He rolled up his blanket and gathered up his utensils and stuffed them into his empty saddle-bags, his guts churning for food and drink. He didn't even have the remains of his whiskey. The bastard had taken that too.

So he was in a vile mood as he journeyed on. He found a stream and dismounted and drank side by side with the mare. It filled a hollow in his belly which wouldn't last long and then rode on.

Suddenly he was aware of shots far ahead. They came in quick succession faintly on the breeze. Tom spurred the mare, a hollow feeling in him which had nothing to do with lack of food.

His headlong gallop brought him to the head of the narrow pass where he'd paused and waved at Rosie when he'd seen her for the last time.

Now, he could see the cabin with its plume of smoke going straight up into the sky. He could also see a horse, tethered beside a watertrough. But all was quiet, and yet the door was open as if someone inside was watching and waiting for whoever would come riding in.

His blood ran cold, for he had just seen a crumpled mass across the threshold.

He looked about him. There was no way he could approach the cabin except by the faint trail ahead. The land was open, pastureland, good for a herd of horses, but bad for an assault on the cabin and its corrals.

He saw the small herd of wild horses and knew they were his only chance. He left the trail and worked around them and then when he was near enough to closeherd them, he gave a Confederate yell and they lifted their heads and squealed and with tails flying high, they stampeded down into the valley and Tom followed close behind.

The herd galloped on, but Tom had gained his objective. He was now behind the rickety barn. Dropping down from his mare, he hobbled her and ran round the barn to watch the front of the cabin.

He waited. He could now see that the crumpled figure was the body of a man. He felt a certain relief. It might have been Rosie.

Then he heard a woman's scream. It was long drawn out and he didn't need a good imagination to know what was happening. He took a chance. If whoever was inside with Rosie was intent on raping her, then Tom had a good chance of surprising him. He took the cleared space in front of the cabin at a run. Colt at the ready. He could hear the sounds of furniture overturning, the slap of hands and the dull thunk of punches followed by grunts. Then he was in the doorway and saw the woman, clawing and spitting, and the enraged man, bleeding profusely from his cheek and growling like a wild beast.

Tom fired a shot into the ceiling. For one shocked moment, all was still and then the man whipped Rosie in front of him. She sagged, but he held her up with cruel firmness.

'Shoot me and you shoot her!' His high pitched giggle stopped Tom in his tracks. 'You never suspected I knew about this bitch, did you, Tom? I knew as soon as we headed for this country just why you turned back from Abilene. I've waited a long time to see your face, Tom, and to know I got here first!'

Tom swallowed and lowered his gun, still stunned to see Josh Kirby alive and kicking.

'But you don't seem to have had any luck with her!' he managed to drawl with a hint of derision in his tone.

Josh scowled. 'You watch yourself, Tom.

You're lucky I let you live! I could have killed you many times over, but that wouldn't have been any good, would it? Not knowing you were being killed because of Ben and all those bloody insults you gave me. I wanted you to know and when I realized...' He looked at Rosie and then giggled. 'Ben always wondered why you wanted us out of this valley so fast. I could have told him, but I wanted it to be *my* secret. I didn't often put one over on Ben but I did that time.' He sounded like a pleased child.

'So what do we do now, Josh? You look a bit tied up, what with holding on to a wildcat and pointing a gun at her. Why don't I just shoot you in the head and be done with it?'

'Because you know the minute you raise that shooter of yours, I'll do for her! That's why!'

'Go on then, shoot her, and I'll get you afterwards!'

Josh looked shocked, and Tom stared at

Rosie as if he'd never seen her before. Inside, he curled up at the look of contempt on her face.

'You mean you don't care? I thought you was the one who preached about lovin' your neighbours and all that crap.'

Tom shrugged. 'A man can make mistakes. I made a mistake with you.'

Josh straightened. 'Yeh? In what way? You mean you wish we'd been proper pards? It's Ben's fault we weren't, wasn't it, Tom?'

'I wasn't thinkin' on those lines, Josh. I was thinkin' I should have made sure I killed you!'

Josh bared his teeth, face flushing.

'You left me for dead but I fooled you! It took me as long as it did you to recover and I did it alone without a woman's help. I'm tougher than you ... a better lover and faster than you with a gun!'

'Prove it, Josh. Let's go outside and prove it once and for all. You can always have Rosie afterwards. She's not goin' to run anywhere...'

Josh looked doubtfully at Rosie and back at Tom.

'You foolin' me, Tom?'

'No. Why should I, Josh?'

'You mean you're willin' to stand up to me, even though I'm goin' to kill you?'

'That's what you want, isn't it, Josh? Or you would have backshot me long before now. You want me to see it in your eyes, don't you, Josh? That very moment when the slug slams into me. You want me to know that it was you, Josh Kirby, the great gunslinger who blasted me in revenge for your brother's killin'. You're so much superior to the rest of us.'

'By God, you sonofabitch, you've got the size of it! I'm glad you know who really was the clever one. Ben kept me down but I knew all along. He said I couldn't survive without him. Well, I've proved it now, haven't I? Go on, admit it!'

'Yeh, you survived, boy.'

'Don't call me that!' he screamed. 'I'm a man and I've had women to prove it, and

I'm goin' to have this one when I finish with you!'

'But you're hangin' on to her as if you daren't let go, Josh. Fasten her to that chair and let's get at it!'

Josh looked from Tom to Rosie and then at the chair.

'You're trying to trap me. You'll blow me to hell while I tie her up. I know you for a sly bastard, Tom. You don't catch me like that!'

'Then what will you do?'

'This.' Suddenly Josh's gun flashed upwards and downwards and Tom heard the sickening coldcocking crunch of a gunbarrel on the back of Rosie's head.

She slumped to the floor and Josh fanned his gun in an arc. It blasted and would have taken Tom's head from his shoulders if he hadn't instinctively dropped to the floor.

Then he took his time. Coldly and deliberately he took aim as Josh's gun clicked on an empty barrel. He shot Josh like he would shoot a mad steer. He put four slugs in him before Josh's body ceased to kick. Then he threw the gun from him. It would be the last time he would kill a man.

He gathered Rosie up in his arms and laid her on the bed, covering her and the remains of her clothing with a blanket. He stoked the stove and carried Josh outside and then examined the body by the door.

It was of a middle-aged man and Tom figured it was Rosie's father. There was a rifle beside the body but it had not been fired. Josh hadn't given the man a chance.

He dragged the corpse outside and laid him alongside Josh. Then he cleared up the mess so that Rosie would not see the mayhem when she opened her eyes.

She was quite a while before she came round and when she did, she cringed and Tom didn't know whether it was the light on her eyes or the sight of himself.

She put a hand to her head and tried to sit up. He gently pushed her back against the pillow.

'What happened?' Her voice was weak.

'He hit you, but you'll be all right. Do

you remember me?'

She peered up at him.

'You're the bastard who told him to shoot me.'

'I'm sorry about that. I knew he wouldn't, because I knew he would never let a woman go until he'd had his rocks off, beggin' your pardon for bein' so blunt.'

A faint pink came up into her cheeks. Then her face clouded. 'My pa … is he…?'

'I'm sorry. He never knew what hit him.'

Suddenly she was crying and clinging to him.

'There's no one left now but me. My grandparents and brother shot last year, and now Pa! What am I goin' to do?'

Suddenly her head came up and she stared at him.

'It's your eyes! I recognize your eyes! You're the man who made me hide! You've come back!' Now she was sobbing all the more.

He held her tightly.

'I'm sorry. It's my fault. I led him back

here. I thought he was dead and I wanted to see if you were safe, and now this has happened,' he said, as he rocked her against him, filled with revulsion at himself. He wanted to vomit.

He felt her stiffen and then relax.

'You mean you came all the way back for me?'

'Yeh. I kept rememberin' you and it was like a heavy black cloud, thinkin' that you might be all alone. I had to make sure. I'm sorry. I should have just put you into my past.'

For a long time they said nothing and then embarrassedly he put her from him.

'I must be goin'.'

'And you would leave me alone after what's happened?'

Tom raised his head. Hell! That was why he had returned because he thought she might be alone! Now what to do?

He gave her a long level glance.

'Do you want me to stay? You know nothing about me. I might be as bad as Josh.

I was a Confederate soldier and I did things that still give me nightmares.'

'I don't care. You were kind to me. You saved my life.'

'But I'm too old for you and I'm an ugly bastard. If I stayed, I'd want you to share my bed. Could you do that?'

She blinked wet eyes.

'We could be friends first. We could find out about each other. I've got a bad temper. Pa says … said I needed a man to paddle my arse.' Her voice wobbled at the mention of her pa. 'Please … please stay. I'm a good cook and I can wash and iron real good and I'm the best at milking cows, so Pa said…' And now her voice dwindled to a whisper. 'Just be kind to me. I can't stay here alone and I have nowhere else to go.'

Tom took a deep breath. Well, this was the dream he'd had in his heart for a long time. A secluded valley, a herd of wild horses, a ready-built home which could be improved when the kids came along. What more did a wise man want?

Tom was a wise man.

He gathered Rosie up close. Her heart beat fast like a bird's. He hugged her close, then still being wise, he put her from him.

'I'll go dig some graves. Where's your folks?'

White-faced now, Rosie took his hand. 'I'll show you.'

Tom nodded. 'You do that, and while I'm doin' the diggin', you cook the biggest steak you can find, for my guts is all wore out for want of food. You can do that?'

Rosie smiled and nodded. 'Yes, I can do that, and anything else you want.'

'The steak will do for starters. I'll think of somethin' for later, but first things first. We've all the time in the world...'

The publishers hope that this book has given you enjoyable reading. Large Print Books are especially designed to be as easy to see and hold as possible. If you wish a complete list of our books please ask at your local library or write directly to:

Dales Large Print Books
Magna House, Long Preston,
Skipton, North Yorkshire.
BD23 4ND